WHEN THE PLUG HAS A
THING FOR YOU

TOY

D1521626

Text **LEOSULLIVAN** to **22828** to join our mailing list!
To submit a manuscript for our review, email us at
submissions@leolsullivan.com

© 2017
Published by Leo Sullivan Presents
www.leolsullivan.com

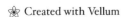 Created with Vellum

CHAPTER 1
ZINDA

"You do know he's gonna hunt your ass down, right?" Key asked me.

I nodded my head up and down because she was right. Juma was gonna come find me, I already knew that. It didn't matter to me because this move had to be done. I needed to get away from everyone, especially him, because no one knew I was pregnant. Getting pregnant was never in the picture. As far as I knew, I couldn't get have kids. Yet, here I am, almost three weeks late with no signs of a period coming anytime soon. I hadn't taken a test yet, but I knew what the fuck the deal was. I had started feeling queasy at random times of the day. I even had to throw out some of the Plug-In air fresheners because they were bothering me.

I didn't even tell Key because she damn sure would tell Sphynx. She didn't know where I was going either. Once I got settled in Florida, I would call her, but not from a traceable phone. I knew all the shit they could do to find out where I was, and I had to use that knowledge to my advantage. I was trying not to be found until after I had the baby, so I had to stay one step ahead of Juma's crazy ass.

"Juma will go on with life after a few weeks of not being able to find me. I'm sure I'm not even on his radar like that. We haven't been talking lately," I told her.

I didn't know if I was supposed to be convincing me or her with that statement. I knew that nigga wasn't gonna give up on finding me. All I could do was hope and pray that he waited to find me until after I had the baby. That's another reason why I was leaving so fast. I needed to get out of there before I started showing.

"Don't come calling me when that nigga kidnaps your ass. You know he will if you push him that far. He loves you. I don't know why you insist on acting like he doesn't. Where are you going? How can I check on you?" Key said.

"I'll call you twice a week. You don't have to worry, I have everything worked out. I have an apartment and a job ready for me when I get there," I explained.

"I don't understand why the fuck you leaving in the first place. You need to stay here so we can all be sure you're okay. I know you know how to take care of yourself, but you still gonna be wherever you going by yourself. I don't like that shit. You know there could still be some shit with your so-called dad. You need to think about this shit some more instead of just up and running off," Key said.

"Your dad is not looking for us or concerned with how we're doing. He's not gonna jump stupid, and you know it. He better be glad his old ass is still breathing," I told her.

She may be worried about him, but he was the last thing on my mind. Her just mentioning him made me want to go to his house and kill him on my way out of town. I knew she wouldn't like us being apart, but she was just gonna have to deal with it. I made my decision already. This was best for everyone. Change is always hard but very necessary. Unfortunately, I would have to deal with the change and looking over my shoulder for Juma to jump his stupid ass out of the bushes.

∞∞∞∞∞∞∞∞

THE DRIVE TO FLORIDA FROM VIRGINIA WAS THE LONGEST drive ever. It didn't help that I was alone and pregnant. If I wasn't stopping to pee, I was stopping to eat. If I could avoid it,

I would never take that drive again. I pulled up to my condo complex just after the sun came up. I was wired from the energy drinks, coffee, and candy that I had been eating. Instead of pulling everything out of the car now, I just locked it up and went to the condo. I thanked God that my furniture had been delivered already. The property manager had let the delivery guys in, so the house was partially set up. I had to put my finishing touches on everything, but I was fine with that as long as I didn't have to move any furniture around.

Once I got in the condo, I laid across the sofa. I was too tired to make it to the bedroom, so I was fine with the sofa for now. I got myself comfortable and drifted off to sleep. I had a ton of shit to do, but it could wait. I didn't start my job for another week, so I had time.

My much-needed rest was interrupted by a knock at the door. I looked at my phone, which was lying on the floor in front of the sofa, and it read seven thirty at night. I had slept the day away, but I felt like I still needed more sleep.

"May I help you?" I said with all the attitude my tired ass could muster up.

I almost had to pause my words. There was a nice, tall, light skin nigga with waves for days on the other side of the door. He had muscles and tattoos all over his chest, which didn't have a shirt over it. That combined with the basketball shorts and slides he had on were doing a number on my concentration. I had to get myself together because this nigga thought he was slick. Why the hell would he be coming to my door dressed liked this?

"You left your keys in the door knob," he said.

He held my keys up between us.

I put my head down to gather my thoughts.

"Thanks. You didn't make any copies, did you?" I asked.

"Nah, I never take what's not given to me willingly, shawty. I was just coming back from the gym, and I saw 'em in the door. Let ya man know if he needs some help getting you unpacked, I'm right next door. My name is Larenzo," he said and put the keys into my hand.

His hands were soft as baby shit. I looked at my hand inside his for a few minutes before I snatched my hand back. I didn't need a new nigga in my life right now, so I had to cut this short.

"Nice try. I don't have a man. I just have a few things in my car that need to be brought in here, so although I appreciate the offer, I won't be needing your assistance," I told him.

"Well, if you ever do, with your independent ass, I'm right next door. It don't matter how late it is, I'm usually up late as fuck anyway. I didn't catch your name, beautiful," he said.

"That's because I didn't throw it. You can call me Anna Mae," I said with a smirk.

"You don't look like no fucking Anna Mae, but I'll call you whatever you want me to. If I call you that bullshit, are you gonna call me Ike?" Larenzo said with a smirk of his own.

I had some sexy light skin trouble living next door to me. I shook my head and laughed at him as I closed the door. I had to get my mind together. The last thing I need was a new nigga in my life right now. Juma's ass had my heart with him. I couldn't be the woman or the mother to his child that he deserved, so I came down here to have the baby and place the child up for adoption.

That's the main reason why I didn't tell anyone about me being pregnant. I knew they would all try to talk me out of it, but it was best for all of us. The kid had me and Juma flowing through their veins, and that is the worst combination ever.

I didn't want to end up like my parents or even fuck up my kid the way my folks had fucked me up. Key didn't go through all the shit I went through because I took a lot of the heat for her. I was actually relieved to find out I couldn't have kids because that meant I didn't have the opportunity to fuck up anyone's life. Now to find out that I'm pregnant as fuck makes me want to go find the doctor who told me I couldn't have kids and torture the motherfucker. Just when I got used to the idea, here comes Juma with his super sperm making the impossible possible.

I went down to the car to get some of the stuff out. On the second trip up, I had to stop and use the wall of the building to get my balance. My head was spinning, and I felt like I was floating. I didn't have time for this right now. Then, out of nowhere,

I threw up in the bushes. It wasn't until I saw the ugly, yellow liquid hit the bushes that I realized I hadn't eaten a damn thing.

"Yo, you good?" I heard Larenzo say from behind me.

"Yeah, I just forgot to eat today. Are you the neighborhood watch or something? Can you please stop looking at my ass?" I asked.

I could feel his eyes on me while I was still bent over dry heaving. That was the most painful shit ever. My eyes were watering, stomach was cramping, and my head was starting to hurt. I was only about five minutes pregnant, and this baby was already making my life a living hell.

"I can't help it. You got that thang poking all at my ass and shit. Do you have some ginger ale or something at your place? That always helped my sister when she was knocked up," he said.

I stood up slowly and rolled my eyes at him. How did he come to that conclusion so quick?

"How do you know I'm pregnant?" I asked.

"It's either you're pregnant or your body is sick because you need a hit of whatever you addicted to. You don't look like an addict, so that leaves you being knocked up with some nigga's kid," he said.

I tried to walk, but my legs were weak. The next thing I knew, he had scooped my ass up and was walking me up the steps. I wanted to argue with him, but I didn't have the energy. I laid my head on his shoulder and prayed that he wasn't on no bullshit.

He took me in the house and put me on the sofa.

"Thank you," I told him softly.

"You got any family here?" he asked.

"No," I answered.

"Where you from?"

"Virginia," I replied.

He looked at me with the side eye. It looked like he wanted to say something, but he didn't. He got up and started looking in my kitchen.

"You pregnant, right? So, why you don't have no food in this motherfucker? All you have is water in here. Since you don't have no family here, I guess I'm your fucking brother from here on

5

out. Everybody needs some friends in their lives. So, I'll agree to be your savior," he said with a smile.

He pulled out his phone and started texting.

"Brothers can't look at their sister's ass like you were looking at mine," I said.

"Shit, a nigga ain't gay. How many niggas you walk past and they don't look? If they not looking at your ass, them niggas gay. We weren't brother and sister then either. I would try my hand with you, but I can tell you got some shit with you. I'll just be the brother because I don't need those problems," he said.

"What you mean?" I asked.

"Well, since you asked. You drove down here by yourself from Virginia. You got a phone here that doesn't have one missed call. You got some burner phones on the table. I know you got family somewhere. You either running from them or the nigga that knocked you up. You don't have no bruises or shit like that, so that means you running for another reason. I got four sisters, so I know how extra and emotional chicks get when they knocked up. So, as long as the nigga you running from don't come wrong when he finds you, everything will be good," he said.

"How you know he looking for me?" I asked.

"Put it like this. If I was that nigga and you had my seed inside you, I would hunt your ass down. Is your cable hooked up?" he asked.

"No, not till Wednesday," I told him.

"Call them and cancel that shit. I got an extra black box, and I can hook up to your TV," he said.

Without waiting for me to agree with him, he got up and went out the door. He came back a few minutes later with a box and a remote in his hand. While he was hooking up the box, there was knock at the door. He opened it, and there were two niggas with grocery bags in their hands.

"Who are they?" I asked.

"These my niggas. I had them go pick up some shit, so you won't be in here starving my nephew," he said.

I got up to help them put up the food. I'd known this nigga for all of ten minutes, but he had niggas out there shopping for me.

"Anna Mae, sit your ass down. Let them niggas get that shit," Larenzo said.

"Damn, Zo, you not gonna introduce us?" one of the guys said.

"Fuck nah, this is lil' sis right here. She off limits to all y'all niggas, so stop acting thirsty. Her nigga will be here soon, and I don't wanna have to help him kill your ass. She Beyonce to y'all niggas. You can dream about her, jerk off thinking about her, but as soon as you touch her, that's your ass. Fuck with it if you want to. Spread the word too, nigga. You know I don't like repeating myself," Larenzo told him.

I shook my head because I knew right then that I was cursed. I was trying to get away from Juma, and I ended up living next to a nigga who acted just like him.

CHAPTER 2

JUMA

"I KNOW YOU HEAR ME KNOCKING ON THIS FUCKING DOOR, ZINDA!" I yelled.

After leaving Mrs. Loretta's house, I rode around for a little while just thinking about if Zinda was pregnant or not. I didn't remember strapping up with her at all. Finally, I called her a few hours ago for the stupid ass operator to tell me that the number was disconnected. I went by all the spots she hung at, even to the fucking chink spot where she got her nails and shit done, only to come up with nothing. I got tired of riding around and looking for her, so I ended up at her damn door.

She had all the fucking time I was willing to give. Now, she got me out there banging on her door like I'm some fucking mad man or something. I finally said fuck it and started kicking the damn door. After the sixth kick, the door flew open. As soon as the door opened, and I saw that mother fucking living room empty, I wanted to faint. My stomach started feeling funny and shit. I walked through the house, and the whole fucking place was empty as fuck.

I left out of the house and headed straight for Key and Sphynx's house. If anybody knew where she went, Key's short ass would know. I drove like a bat out of hell to their house. My tires squealed as I threw my car into park in front of the house and hopped out with it still running. I knocked on the door hard as hell.

Key came to the door with her face all balled up, but I didn't give one solid fuck. I was ready to snap somebody's fucking neck.

"Where's your sister?" I asked her.

"I don't know. She didn't tell me where she was going either," she said.

"And you just let her go without fucking knowing where she was going? She's alone wherever she is. That shit don't bother you? I know she told you where she went. Go 'head and tell me," I yelled.

"What the fuck is going on out here? What the fuck is up with your ass hollering at her like that?" Sphynx came out of nowhere.

"Man, Zinda's gone. Key won't tell me where the fuck she is," I told him.

"What the fuck you mean gone?" he asked.

Sphynx had his face all balled up looking between me and his pregnant wife. I knew there was a chance that I was gonna have to fight this big, black mother fucker, but I was here for it.

"I went to her house, and the shit is empty as fuck. She done moved on a nigga. She didn't even leave a fucking sock in her place. Every fucking thing is gone. It don't even look like anybody lived in that motherfucker," I told him.

"Where is she, Key?" he asked.

"I don't fucking know. She wouldn't tell me," she said and hunched her shoulders.

"She wouldn't tell you, and you didn't think to at least tell one of us? We could've had somebody tailing her to make sure she was good. Y'all think y'all that damn bad because you can box a little bit and break down a gun. What she gonna do if somebody run up on her in the middle of the night? Any fucking thing can happen. I hope your fucking secrets don't lead to her getting hurt. If it does, I'm kicking your pregnant ass, Key," Sphynx fussed.

"How you gonna threaten me when I'm carrying your fucking baby? You say what the fuck you want. I was doing what she asked me to do. Don't stand there and act like if this nigga wanted to get away that you wouldn't keep it to yourself if he asked you to. Y'all got life fucked up if you think I'm gonna feel bad for holding my sister down," Key argued back to Sphynx.

"Make sure you write all that shit down when your riding for her gets her ass killed. You make sure you say all that shit you just said with all the same fucking emotion. It's not about you riding for her or selling her ass out. Her ass could be in danger. Y'all too busy playing hide and seek to see the bigger picture," he told her.

"We don't know about any beef in the street. I guess I'm not the only one keeping shit to myself," she said, giving Sphynx the side eye.

"You not involved in this street shit no more. Why you need to know any fucking thing? Don't side eye me like that. This street shit don't concern you no more. You don't need to know shit. Let me find out one of them niggas telling you shit, Imma kill his ass. You my wife now, and you carrying my child. Act like it," he told her.

I was pacing back and forth as they fussed. I needed Zinda to be safe, and I couldn't protect her if I didn't know where she was. Beef could come up at the drop of a dime these days. Although, we got most of the shit settled, all of it wasn't. I'm sure if somebody wanted to come at me, she would be the first thing they fucking attack. I needed to at least have some eyes on her that I could trust.

"Getting back to the fucking point. Why the fuck didn't you tell me she fucking moved? You know better than anybody that Juma in the streets, and the first thing they gonna go for is her ass to get to him. I thought you were smarter than that, Key. I see why this nigga 'bout to go the fuck off. He got every right to," Sphynx told her.

She started crying, but right now her tears didn't mean shit to me. I was too worried about my future wife's safety. I hauled ass to the bathroom and threw up in the toilet. I had been feeling like I was coming down with something, but I hadn't thrown up since I was a fucking kid.

Sphynx came to the bathroom behind me.

"You good, nigga? What the fuck you throwing up for? The only time my ass threw up was when Key's ass was knocked up. You got somebody's daughter knocked up, nigga," he said with a smile.

What the hell is going on today? Why it seems like the words pregnant, baby, and knocked up were following my ass. First Mrs. Loretta, and now this nigga. Zinda hadn't said shit to me, so I wasn't claiming shit. It's been a month since I been up in her, so maybe she didn't know shit yet. I was nervous as hell, but I wasn't gonna let Sphynx ass know. I know I needed to find her to get some answers, though.

"Fuck you, nigga. If I had a kid on the way, I would know. Besides, since me and your sister-in-law been beefing, I just been getting topped off. Throats don't get pregnant, motherfucker," I told his ass.

"Nigga, say what you want. You knocked somebody up," Sphynx said.

After I finished spilling my guts, I rinsed my mouth out with water then used the Scope mouthwash they had on the back of the sink. I heard what he was saying, but the only person I fucked with like that was Zinda's runaway ass. Like I said before, she hadn't said shit to me about being pregnant, so I paid his ass no mind.

Then I thought about it. She didn't say anything about moving either. I walked back to the living room.

"How are you supposed to keep in contact with her?" I asked Key.

"Huh?" she said.

"Answer the question. I'm wondering the same shit," Sphynx told her.

"She's gonna call me from a burner phone," Key answered.

"A fucking burner phone? What the fuck did I do so damn bad for her to be moving like she on the run? What the fuck is really going on?" I asked.

For her to go to all these damn extremes made me think something else was going on with her. Why would she up and run? What the hell was she running from? All I wanted to do was show her how a queen was supposed to be loved and treated.

There had to be something going on that we were all missing. There was a reason for this shit, I just had to find her and try to figure this shit out.

"Is your sister pregnant with my seed?" I asked Key.

"If she is, she didn't tell me about it. She just said that she needed to start over. I tried to talk her out of it, but she left anyway," she said through her tears.

I guess her and Sphynx were beefing now behind this disappearing act of Zinda's. Sphynx was side-eying the fuck out of her right now. She didn't understand that she was putting herself in danger moving like this. I figured she couldn't be too damn far because after all, she was by herself. That wasn't my problem right now.

I got tired of going back and forth with Key. It was obvious she didn't know shit because if she did, she would have told Sphynx. Key could play hard and lie to everyone but Sphynx.

I left their house without saying goodbye. I had to figure out what my next move was. I needed to find Zinda, and I needed to find her ass quick.

I had to relieve some tension so I could think straight. I decided to call Cherry. Cherry was what I called a top off queen. The damn girl could suck an orange through a coffee straw. She was always available when I needed her ass. She wasn't Zinda, but she would do. I wasn't fucking her, and she was cool with sucking me off, swallowing, and going about her merry way.

"Hello," she answered.

"I'm on my way. Get that mouth right," I told her before ending the call.

There wasn't a need to have any further conversation. I didn't care about her. She served a purpose, and that was to suck and swallow. I didn't care what she did with other niggas. A few times I came to her house, and another nigga was leaving out. I always threw the nigga a head nod and kept it moving. I don't know what she told him to make his ass leave, and I didn't give a fuck. I was only gonna be there for twenty minutes tops. Maybe she had that nigga ride around the block or some shit.

I pulled up to her house, and this time she was standing in the door with a small ass robe on. I guess everyone in her hood knew what she was about because they were paying her ass no mind. I shook my head because there was no fucking way that Zinda would stand in the door like that. This is why Cherry would never be a priority for any real nigga out here. I thought to myself, *if that was Zinda looking like, that I would fuck her 'til she couldn't fucking walk.*

When I got up to the door, she smiled and opened the full glass screen door with a smile on her face. As I walked in, she licked her big ass lips, which made my dick hard on the spot. She turned to walk to her room, I guess, but, I wasn't with that today. I just needed her to get this shit over with so I could start looking for Zinda.

"Nah, right here," I told her.

She looked at me then at the glass screen door that was open. She looked kind of hesitant. Now was not the time for her to be acting all shy and shit. She had sucked me off in a fucking drive-thru before, so I knew she didn't give a fuck if people saw her. Knowing her trick ass, the audience probably turned or on. I remember that blowjob that day had me contemplating actually buying her some food. Of course, I changed my mind when she was done. The only food she could get from me was my nut.

"The door is open," she said.

"Either close it or leave it open, I don't care. You act like don't nobody know why I'm here. Everybody knows you Super-head on a budget out here in these streets. So, don't act like you haven't sucked a nigga off in front of other people before. I know you remember that night in the drive-thru. That's basically the same shit. I just need my dick in your mouth. All that other shit I don't give a fuck about," I told her.

She dropped to her knees and got to work. My eyes closed and my head fell back as she worked her magic. Any other time, my mind would be clear, but today I was thinking about Zinda, and all the ways I could punish her pussy for dipping out on my ass.

CHAPTER 3

CHERRY

I was dancing at the club like I did six nights a week and hoping that Juma brought his heartbroken ass in there tonight. I had been trying to step up and be the woman that he needed. I know y'all haven't heard about me, but I'm the bitch that's gonna take Zinda's place. Juma has been coming in here a lot more now that they had broken up. Before she came on the scene I was at the top of Juma's list to call when he needed a nut.

Juma is a prime catch; he always has been, really. I've known Juma for a few years now. He was just a middle level dope boy when he and I crossed paths. He used to tell me I was one of his favorites, but now when he sees me, it's always 'get to it,' or 'you know what's up.'

There were nights when he would come in the club, and he would keep me in the champagne room all night just for him. The bitches in there were jelly as fuck because I was his first choice. Some nights the bouncers had to walk me out because these bitches wanted to jump my ass.

I wasn't delusional enough to think that Juma would make me his wife or no shit like that. I would be the perfect Bonnie to his Clyde, though. I had been trying to get him to chill with me a little more. Now that him and his girl had broken up, I was trying to play my cards right. I knew he wasn't going to make an announcement about me like he did her. If I could convince him to at least let me set a few niggas up to get robbed for him or something, he would see how valuable I am to him.

I peeped out of the curtains backstage to see if he was in his crew's usual VIP section, but he wasn't. I had to go out there and act all happy to be with these niggas who weren't making that long money, but they had enough to share. I was on a mission to secure the bag tonight since I couldn't get a piece of Juma.

I saw a few of his lieutenants, so I figured might as well go entertain them. I might get to ride at least two nice sized dicks tonight. I knew Rock, Polo, and Draino all loved the way I wrapped my mouth around their dicks. Depending on how high and drunk they were, I could find out about Juma and Zinda. One thing those niggas did when they were lit was talk. When they talked they didn't put a limit on what type of info they would give.

Just by entertaining them, I was sure to leave with five G's just from them niggas. I walked over to them with a smile on my face and an extra twist in my ass.

"Do you gotta go on stage tonight, Cherry?" Polo asked me.

"Nope, I'm all yours tonight if you want me to be," I answered.

They all looked at each other and started laughing.

"Is Juma coming up here tonight?" I asked.

"Shit, that nigga too busy running down behind black ass Zinda to do anything," Draino said.

"I don't know what kind of pussy she got, but I don't want no parts of it. That nigga been on one since she up and left," Polo said.

I sat on Draino's lap and fixed myself a drink while they talked. I was just waiting for some info that I could use to come up. I couldn't believe that Juma was running down behind that bitch. She didn't appreciate the shit he did for her. If I was him, I would cut my losses and come get with a real bitch like me. I started dancing in front of Draino to make them think I was in my own world.

"That nigga gonna fuck around and somebody gonna come knock his ass off his pedestal. I can't wait, either. That nigga swears he the smartest nigga out here. The only reason he got the position he in now is because Serion and Sphynx are doing the family thing. It ain't like he earned this shit. He was just the next in line," Rock said.

"Oh yeah, tell that nigga all that in his face. I bet money your ass won't do it," Polo told Rock.

"Nigga, I'm not trying to die yet," Rock said and laughed.

"Since y'all niggas too busy over here talking. I'm gonna take her off y'all hands. Unless y'all niggas wanna train track her ass tonight. You know she get excited about that shit with her hoe ass," Polo said.

He pulled me over to him and held me close as he bent his head to lick my exposed cleavage. I let my head fall back and enjoyed the feeling he was giving me. He squeezed my ass then gave it a smack.

"You down for a train ride tonight?" Polo asked.

"You know I'm down for whatever. I need something to do anyway. Why not ride some of my favorites?" I whispered in his ear.

"We 'bout to be your only favorites because that nigga Juma 'bout to be on his way out. If I had some help, I would take over my damn self," Draino said.

"Nigga, we trying to slide up in some pussy, and you worrying about that nigga. Let me find out you out here crushing on his ass," Rock said.

"Neva that. I just want Cherry here to know that she's fucking with the next three kings of the seven cities. She need to be down with a real team," Draino said.

Draino was always trying to make himself look more impor-tant than he really was. I used to think he was jealous of Juma and how he came up in the game. Now, I'm not too sure. It was more that he wanted to be at the top, but he didn't want to put in the work to get there. He was more of an 'I'll just take it' type of nigga.

We got into the room. I was ready to make some money, so as soon as the door closed I dropped to my knees to do what I was known for. The whole time I was in the room with them, I was picturing Juma as the one I was with. I was sure not to call out any specific name, though. That's something you learn early in the game. If you called out the wrong name, that could make a guy beat your ass. I didn't need those problems.

"You really trying to get down with the team, huh?" Polo asked me.

My night with them was finally over. I don't know how long we were in the room, but my body was sore. Draino and Rock had left me in the room with Polo.

"If I ever get down with any type of team; I have to be the queen. I'm a rider, but I also have the mind of a hustler. If you're ever looking for a rider who will put in work beside you, then I'm your chick. This stripping thing is just a means to an end," I told him.

"Nobody will ever know that if all you do is stick the closest dick in your mouth. You can't talk with your mouth full. Real shit, I'm putting some shit together that nobody knows about. If I need your help, I'll let you know. Just make sure you don't come with a bunch of excuses when the time comes," Polo told me.

I nodded my head and walked to the locker room. I need a good night's sleep so I could dream about Juma and I taking over. I packed up and left the building.

Once I got home, I fixed me a drank, ran my bubble bath, and tried to relax. My phone rang, which wasn't odd that it was ringing at five in the morning. I just wasn't in the mood to be fucking anybody right now. I saw that it was my cousin, Kenny, so I answered it. I knew he was probably calling to tell me that he was gay or something.

Kenny wasn't a regular type of man. He claimed he had girl-friends, but none of the family had ever seen one of them. He was a cool guy, but he was creepy, even to me, and I'm family.

"Hey, cuz," I answered.

"Do you know a chick named Zinda?" he asked quickly.

I knew damn well there aren't too many Zindas in the world. That name was all fucked up, so I knew she had to be the only one.

"Is she dark skinned and bowlegged?" I asked.

"Yeah, that's her. She just started at my job. Cuz, when I tell

TOY

you she's gonna be my wife, that's what the fuck I mean. She's got my full attention out here, ya heard," he told me.

I rolled my eyes because here he goes with the bullshit.

"You and her dating?" I asked.

"No, not yet, but we're getting close. She told me she was from Virginia. Then one day she told me exactly where she was from," he said.

"Did you tell her you had family here?" I asked.

"No, I basically just listened to her talk about her leaving home because she needed a change. I could listen to her talk all day and never get bored," he said.

"Damn, cuz. She got you open like that? Well, I say if you all into her, you should try your hand with her. You're a good man, and you deserve to be happy," I told him.

"You right. I just want to give her the world," Kenny said.

"Well, then, you do that. Don't let nothing hold you back, either. You do everything in your power to make her understand that you are what she needs," I told him.

"Thanks, cuz. I gotta get ready to go to work. I'll call you in a few days to let you know what's going on," Kenny said.

We ended the call. All I could do was laugh. Zinda had no idea what she was in for. Knowing my cousin, he was gonna stalk the fuck outta her. That was good for me because I needed her to be focused on somebody else. I needed her to forget all about my bae, Juma.

CHAPTER 4
KEY

I hope that damn girl knew what the hell she was doing. She got me in here getting the side eye from this crazy nigga behind her shit. Juma had been gone for a few hours, but he was still on the shit. I mean, what the fuck did he expect? I'm my sister's keeper, and she is mine. Nothing is gonna change that, husband or not, he got me fucked up.

"You sure she not pregnant?" Sphynx asked me.

"She didn't say anything about being pregnant. If she did, I would have tried harder to stop her," I told him.

"But you just let her go because she was in her fucking feelings. That makes a lot of fucking sense. If something happens to her, I'm gonna blame your apple head ass. If she pregnant, then you gonna be next, no bullshit," Sphynx said.

"What her being pregnant got to do with me? That don't even sound logical. How you holding me responsible for someone else's actions? You sound stupid right now," I told him.

"I'm not a logical type of nigga. What the fuck you thought? The point is, you should have told me what the fuck was going on. I told your ass about secrets and shit. I tell your ass everything, and you should do me the same way. We can't be a unit if you being all slick and shit," he said.

I couldn't say much because everything he said was right. I should have said something to him, but that would put me in a bind with her. I was stuck in the middle right now. I needed to find a way to get things right with my husband.

"Bae, real shit, I didn't want to tell you because I was being loyal to my sister. She didn't want anyone to know she was leaving. You have to understand that. You still haven't told me what was going on in the street. Why that's not the same thing? You got your secrets, and I only didn't tell you one damn thing, but I'm the one wrong," I told him.

"I do, but, you need to realize that her leaving just put her in more danger. If I would have known, I would have put a guy on her to keep watch without her knowing. How many fucking times do I have to say that? I got a bad feeling about this.

"When she calls, you have to at least find out what state she in. I can't believe you just went along with this shit, though. I tell you what, though. If we end up beefing, you betta run your ass to the guest room. We not doing that 'split up,' or 'need some time' bullshit. Not on my fucking watch. Try that shit if you want to. I gotta go make some moves. I'll be back in a few," Sphynx told me.

I watched him walk out of the house and slam the door behind him. I knew I had to try to find my sister too if I wanted to stop this beef between Sphynx and me. I didn't know who or what was going on in the streets, but from the way both of them were acting, I knew something had to be going on. The first thing I needed to do was find out what we were up against.

I had some phone calls to make while Sphynx was out. The first call I made was to the guy who made the drops for us when we here counting. He usually stayed in the loop. He had to because he had to know who to keep an eye out for.

"Oh, shit, what happened?" he said as soon as he answered.

I laughed because that's the only thing he would say to me first. It didn't matter if I just said hi to him or if I really had a question for him.

"Why you always gotta say that? I can't call and see how you doing?" I asked.

"Cuz, you only call when you wanna know something. So, what you need? Do Sphynx know you calling me because I don't want those problems?" he said with a laugh.

"I just wanna know what's goin' on in the streets since I been doing the housewife thing," I asked him.

"Well, word on the street is that some nigga on the other side of town got beef with Juma. He been coming by all the spots leaving messages for him and shit. The trip shit is that Juma say he don't know who the hell dude could be. They supposed to meet up next week because the last time, dude never showed up. They were supposed to meet before, so I doubt that dude shows up this time. I think he just likes seeing Juma on edge," he said.

"Nobody know his name or nothing? You still haven't said a name. So, they out here beefing with Batman?" I said.

"Nope. All he says is you know who or some dumb shit like see you in a minute. I doubt it's Batman, being that Batman ain't fucking real, but I get what you saying," he told me as he laughed.

The call waiting beeped on the phone, and I saw that it was an unsaved number. I got off the line with ol' boy and clicked over. I was hoping it was the runaway.

"Hello," I answered.

"Hey, sis. I made it," Zinda said.

"Made it where? Are you pregnant? Juma went by your place and you weren't there. He's pissed, came over here going off on me. Where are you? You need to be careful. It's some street shit going on here, so keep ya head on a swivel," I told her.

"What you mean street shit? Why do I need to keep my head on a swivel? I don't have shit to do with what is going on there. He won't find me anyway. Why you talking so damn fast? I'm good. Whatever Juma has going on out there, he will work it out," her dumb ass said.

"Yeah, alright, you keep believing that shit. You didn't answer me. Is you knocked up?" I asked with a raised voice.

"Huh. What? No, I'm not pregnant. I was just calling to tell you I made it. There's a guy who lives next door, and he's looking out for me. You have an honorary brother down here. He had some guys buy me some food, so I could eat. When I got here, I went to sleep for most of the day," she said.

I could tell by the tone of her voice that she was lying about something. Now, she had me pacing with the phone in my hand. I started rubbing my stomach, which was something I started doing when I got really nervous. I was starting to get a bad feeling, just like Sphynx.

"I need to come where you are. I don't trust that you will be okay. You're there all by yourself. I know you gonna fight me on this, but we don't even know who this guy is that has the beef with Juma. They know how he feels about you just like everybody else around here but you. I shouldn't have just let you go like that. Just tell me where you are, and I'll come down there with you. You gonna make me have a miscarriage fucking with your where's Waldo ass," I told her.

She got real quiet on me. I knew she was there because I could hear her sniffling on the phone. There wasn't a need for her to be crying. She was the one who started all this shit in the first place.

"You can't. If you do, then Juma's gonna know where I am. I can't handle that right now," she cried.

I didn't have time to play with her silly ass right now. It's too damn dangerous for her to be out there alone, and she was playing fucking games.

"Real fucking talk, Zinda, he needs to know where you are. We all need to know where your stupid ass is. You gonna fuck around and have to call us to come save your ass. You say you not pregnant. You say you need a fresh start. You could've had that anywhere, so why did your dingy ass leave the fucking state? What you hiding? What you not telling me? It has to be something because right now you not making sense. How you moving ain't adding up. What you lying about?" I asked her.

She needed to get her shit together. If something happens to her because she's being a jack ass, I'm gonna kick her ass like I didn't know her. I waited for her to respond, but she never did. She ended the call on my ass. I looked at the phone, and even though it was a burner phone, a number still flashed across my screen. I wrote the number down and googled it.

I called Sphynx as soon as the information popped up. He answered the phone but didn't say anything because he's an asshole like that sometimes.

"She called. I googled the number, and she's in Miami, Florida, according to the phone number she called from," I told him.

"Miami? What the fuck she go that far for? Man, this is some bullshit. Do y'all know anybody down that motherfucker?" Sphynx asked.

"No. I guess she needed to go down there so she could get her fresh start," I told him.

Just like I knew he would, he ended the call without a word. I went to lie down because I knew with all the bullshit ahead, I would need to rest while I could.

CHAPTER 5

JUMA

I pulled up in the parking lot beside the information guy's car. I called him the information guy because he didn't let too many people know what his name was. He was paranoid that someone was going to hack into his shit on a computer. I think he was paranoid because of all the shit that he knows he can do with a little bit of information. Whenever I met with him, it was always in an empty ass parking lot. The shit was spooky as fuck to me at first, but after all these years of working with him, he had the trust and respect of the whole crew.

"What's up, Juma?" he asked.

"A bunch of dumb shit going on. What do you have for me?" I asked.

"Sphynx called and told me she was in Miami. He said something about her calling Key. I thought you said she would go somewhere close? Miami is about as far as you can get without a damn boat or plane," he said to me.

"Yeah, that's what she should have done. She got everybody she considers family here. I know she's pissed with me, but she ain't have to move all the way down there," I told him.

"She's in Florida with all their sunshine and beautiful beaches. I'll take that shit over our fucked-up weather any day," he told me.

I didn't care about no fucking beaches or sunshine. She needed to bring her ass home.

"What the fuck she doing in Florida? Who the fuck she down there with?" I barked at him.

He shook his head at me because he knew I wasn't expecting this shit. Florida. Motherfucking Florida. She really wanted me to kick her ass. Who the hell was down there with her?

"From what I could tell, she's working and that's it. She hasn't been going to any clubs or nothing. There's a nigga in her apartment complex who lives next door to her. From what I can tell, he's been helping her out with shit. I don't think he's trying to get with her or nothing. From what I can see, he's just looking out.

"The place where she works, she has a guy that I think is digging her, but that's it. She only sees him when she's at work. I don't think he even knows where she lives, to be honest. She never has any kind of company either besides the guy next door. He usually brings her food or some bullshit like that. He's been taking her car to get washed. It's like he doesn't want her to do anything besides go to work.

"I have her work place in the file along with a picture of the dude. I got a feeling he may be bad news, so if you plan on going down there, keep an eye out for his ass," he told me.

I took the envelope from him and started going through it. It wasn't that I didn't trust homeboy, I just couldn't believe she was in Florida.

"Who's the nigga with his helpful ass?" I asked.

"His street name is Craze Zo. Real name is Larenzo Ortiz. He runs a crew of car thieves and two trap houses. He doesn't have to be in the street, but he loves the shit. He has a mother and four sisters that he looks out for. Doesn't have one main chick, but the nigga has options for days," he said and laughed.

I didn't respond because I was already trying to figure out how I was gonna kill the nigga in my head. I hoped he wasn't on some bullshit with Zinda because I will tie her ass up and make her pee on a fucking stick. If she's pregnant, then I would hold her ass hostage till she had the baby. She could sign her rights over to me and then do whatever the fuck she wanted to do. I knew damn well ain't no random ass nigga gonna just look out for some chick he doesn't know.

"Is the address in here?" I asked him.

"Yeah. Heads up, the building she lives in is up for sale. I don't know how you feel about being a property owner, but it might work in your favor to check into it," he said.

I gave him the head nod. He pulled off, and I sat in the parking lot going through all the info he had on Zinda. There were pictures of her at work and at home. This nigga was thorough as fuck when it came to finding people. I had her bank accounts listed and everything. He did a hell of a job with this one. This nigga even threw in a couple of red light pictures.

He was right about the guy smiling all in her face at work. The nigga who lived next door looked like Nelly. You know, all buff and shit. I knew I was gonna have to kill his ass for damn sure.

I started the car and went straight to Sphynx's house. Key was about to catch all this frustration that was in my head right now. If nobody else knew where Zinda was, I knew her short, butterball turkey looking ass did. I pulled up to the house and hopped out of the car.

Sphynx came to the door before I could knock. I guess he saw me on the monitors.

"What up, J?" he asked.

"I gotta go to Florida. I'm leaving in the morning. You and Key still beefing?" I asked him.

"Fuck yeah. She told me where Zinda was according to the phone she called her from. I just wanna know why she went all the way down there," Sphynx said.

"Same shit I'm saying. You know your baby mama knew where she went and didn't tell nobody. They both still trying to live reckless. She don't have no business down there alone, man. You know how this shit go. If somebody wants to come at us, they gonna go for her because she's an easy fucking target," I fussed.

I was thirty-eight hot because she had no business going all the way down there. If something went down, she was gonna be alone down there. I couldn't have that shit, not on my fucking watch.

"I'm going to pop up on her ass. I'm gonna shock the fuck outta her. You know she hardheaded as fuck. Even when I get there, she's gonna try to justify this dumb ass move she made," I told Sphynx.

"You sure you wanna do that? The last thing you need is to go down there and catch a charge for yoking her ass up," he said.

"Hell yeah," I replied.

I didn't want to say she might be pregnant right now because there was still a chance that she might not be. I know that sometimes those old folks can be wrong, but Mrs. Loretta hasn't been wrong in all the years that I've known her. So, her telling me what she did sealed the deal for me.

"Keep ya head on a swivel. You know those niggas down there don't give a fuck," he told me.

I gave him a head nod and left out. I got on the phone as soon as I shut the car door. My guns shoot just like those motherfuckers.

"Hello," my realtor, Justin, answered.

"Justin, this is Juma. I'm gonna text you an address of an apartment building in Florida that's for sale. I don't care what you have to do, but make sure I'm the owner of it in the next two days," I told him.

"Is there anything else?" Justin asked.

That's why I fuck with Justin. He knows that I don't have time for a bunch of bullshit. I never had to tell him why I wanted to buy something, he just went with the flow. I loved that shit because I hated explaining myself to anybody. Justin was about his money, but he never let me jump into some shit that would have been reckless.

"Yeah, buy up all the apartment buildings on the block while you're at it. Get this shit done by the time I told you, there will be a ten thousand dollar tip for you," I told him.

Yeah, I wasn't playing no games with her ass. I called the pilot we had on call to see when the jet would be available. Just like I thought, he said it would be ready in two days. So, I had

two days to get my shit here in order so I can move my ass to
Florida.

CHAPTER 6
ZINDA

I sat on my balcony just taking in the scenery. The sky was blue, the water was clear, and the world awaited me. This move was something that I needed to do to help me do better. I needed to stand on my own with no one around me to give me grief about my decision.

I looked at the stick that was on the table beside me. I never thought I would be at this point in life. Tears streamed down my face. This was not something I needed in my life right now. I know y'all are wondering why would I take a pregnancy test if I knew I was already pregnant. I took the test because I hadn't taken one yet. I had the symptoms, but now I had the in your face proof. I couldn't deny it anymore or make up some other reason for my symptoms.

I thought about calling in at work, but I didn't because I just got the job. My mind wasn't on that damn job right now. My car was in the shop, and Larenzo wasn't home. I had to break down and call a fucking cab to get to work. I thought about calling this guy named Kenny from work to come get me, but there was something off about him.

I got up because if I sat there any longer, I was going to end up doing something that I didn't need to do. The urge to call Juma was weighing heavily on me. I hadn't made a decision one way or the other yet, so I didn't need to make any calls.

I heard the cab outside honking the horn. I was going to leave the stick at home, but I decided to take it with me. I grabbed my purse and headed out the door as fast as I could with six-inch heels on my feet. Not paying attention, and not expecting anyone to be at my door this early in the morning, I was shocked and a little scared when I saw the back of man on the other side of my door.

"Can I help you with something?" I asked.

"You can take your ass back in the house. You not working today," the man said.

"Juma?" I asked, even though I knew his voice.

"Nice to know you remember me. Now get your ass back in the house," he said, turning around.

He looked down at the stick in my hand.

I dropped it in my purse.

He smiled at me.

"What was that?" he asked.

"None of your business," I told him with as much attitude as I could gather.

"Yo, dog, she good. She doesn't need a ride today," he yelled to the cab driver.

The cab driver pulled off with a smile on his face.

"Whatever we have to discuss, you need to start talking now because I'm not letting you in my apartment," I told him.

"You don't have to. I have a key to all these mother fuckers," he said and laughed.

"What do you mean you have a key to all of them?" I asked.

"I own this motherfucker. The one across the street, and the one next door," he said.

My heart dropped to my feet just that quick. He walked around me and put a key in my door knob. I walked in behind him as he invited himself to my refrigerator.

"Juma! What the hell are you doing?" I asked.

"I'm trying to get some answers from my baby mama. She can either give them to me now, or I can get them later. She needs to know that I'm now a resident of the sunshine state as well. I also stay in the apartment above her. I'm not gonna drill little holes in my floor to stalk her yet, though. You ready to spend the day with your baby daddy?" he asked.

This nigga had gone in my refrigerator and took out my whole bag of grapes. He happily took a seat on my sofa like I asked him to, and was tossing grapes back like he fucking paid for them. Why would he buy up the apartment buildings like that? What the hell was he up too?

"There is no baby, so there is no baby daddy," I told him.

I was trying to sound convincing. If I did that, then maybe he would carry his ass. This is Juma we're talking about. He wasn't going anywhere, and I knew it.

"So, you just piss on sticks for the fun of it, huh? Come on, we going to the clinic, so your ass can get out of denial. You gonna admit that my sperm was straight beasting on your eggs. I told you that you were gonna get pregnant, didn't I? You gonna stop doubting a nigga like me. You ready now, or do you want to change your clothes?" he said to me.

I rolled my eyes up to the sky because he was acting like I was really gonna go somewhere with him. I kissed my teeth and went in my room. My mind was moving a mile a minute. I needed him to leave my apartment. Shit, I needed him to leave the state of Florida all together. How did he find out where I was?

I had been careful not to leave a paper trail. At least I thought I was. Key only knew that I went down south, not my specific location. How the hell did he end up buying the whole fucking building? This was some bullshit.

I felt him come and stand right up on me. My back was to his chest, and I could feel his hard dick against my lower back. He slid his arms around me and placed soft kisses on my neck. My nipples instantly got hard. This was why I needed to get far away from him in the first place. My body had a mind of its own when it came to Juma. Sometimes I could get all juicy and tingly just by him looking at me.

"The more you fight this, the more enticing you are to me. You from the streets, so I have no fucking clue why you so damn scared," he said between kisses.

My eyes closed, and I began to enjoy the closeness of him.

Despite my brain telling me constantly that I was no good for him, this was the man who my body craved and longed for. I dreamed of him nightly. Often, I would reminisce about the times we had together. He was the reason my heart and mind stayed in a constant battle.

I suddenly stepped away from him.

"You need to get out," I told him, fighting back the tears.

CHAPTER 7

JUMA

This damn girl was gonna make me clock the shit out of her. It was already bad enough that I let her have her little time for a whole fucking month. Her time running and time to herself was fucking done. I knew she thought that Key had told me where she was, but she was dead ass wrong. Key didn't tell my ass shit.

"Sphynx had called up the nigga who found Sonnet for Serion and put his ass to work. He gave me all the info on you. He even put me on to the building being up for sale. I ended up buying what was for sale on the block just to be close to you. I know about your little work husband too. Don't worry, I'm not gonna kill his ass now, or should I say yet?" I said and laughed.

"What the hell you talking about? I don't have a work husband. You definitely tripping. I'm not entertaining anybody down here. That's not one of my priorities right now," she said.

"So, when is our child gonna be a priority for you? Fuck all that other shit. When the fuck are you gonna admit to being knocked up by me in the first place? If you ask me, you need to rethink your bullshit ass priorities. I can't wait all day for you to fix your damn life, so we gonna speed up the process. Get ya ass up and come on," I told her.

I thought about how all this shit started to hit me. I started getting sick about two weeks ago. Now, in all my life, so far, I had never been that sick. I can count on my hands how many times I've been sick in my life. So, I was trying to figure out what the hell was going on with me. I went to the doctor and everything. At first, the doctor told me there must have been some type of bug going around. I stayed home for two days trying to get the shit under control.

After Zinda and I started doing this whole break thing that she needed, I had only been getting topped off by chicks. Don't get me wrong, I almost fucked this one chick, but when I looked at her, I started seeing Zinda. I got my ass out of there quick.

There wasn't shit that these other females could do for a nigga like me. I needed my Z back in my life, so that's why I was there, of course, and to see if she was really pregnant. I heard about some guys having the morning sickness instead of the woman. Well, I'm here to tell you that the shit is true as fuck.

Her phone rung, instead of answering it she looked at me.

"What you looking at me for? Answer the damn phone and tell Kenny you got a doctor's appointment that you forgot about. You not going to work today. I know 'bout ya little boyfriend next door too. Me and that nigga got some shit to discuss," I told her.

"Did you hear me tell you to leave?" she asked.

"Yeah, I heard you. Do you see me moving? Answer the damn phone and let the nigga know," I told her.

She answered the phone, and I could hear the nigga acting all concerned about why she wasn't at work yet. The way he was questioning her, you would think that they were in a real relationship.

"Did you kiss that nigga? Has he touched your booty?" I asked her.

"No," she said with her face balled up.

My phone rang. It was Cherry, so I ignored the call. She rolled her eyes acting all dramatic and shit.

"Why you didn't answer your fucking phone? You all in my damn face, but you got bitches calling your phone. Why you so pressed about me?" she asked.

"Because you gonna be my wife. That bitch on the phone just

in love with the angry dick I give her when I'm pissed with you. You know you miss my long stroke," I said.

I was just fucking with her. I still had my control over her body and I knew it. Her nipples were hard, she was nervous because she couldn't keep still. I don't know why she was acting like she was over me.

"Get out," she said.

"You want me to leave so you can go play with that pussy. I know it's wet. That's fucked up you keep denying me of my shit. Just admit it's mine so we can go back to Virginia together," I told her.

"No, Juma, get out," she said.

"I'm not leaving, so you can stop saying that shit. We going to the clinic and we gonna talk the whole ride there, so come on, baby mama," I told her.

I know the term baby mama got on her nerves. It didn't matter though because no matter how much she tried to avoid it or act like it wasn't happening, shawty was about to push out a kid for me. She was taking her time like I knew she would, but I didn't mind. These grapes were banging like a motherfucker. I was gonna end up eating the fucking bag. I was just about to ask her where she got them, but there was a knock at the door. She looked at me when the nigga knocked again.

"What the fuck you looking at me for? I ain't the one at the door. Get the door, Zinda," I told her.

She just kept standing there looking scared to death. I'd never seen her look like that before. The shit was hilarious. I sat back on the sofa and turned the TV on. She could leave his muscle neck ass out there. I didn't care 'bout the nigga. I know damn well she better not care 'bout his ass either.

CHAPTER 8

LARENZO

This damn girl was turning out to be just like my damn sisters. She was supposed to be at work, but I got word that she didn't go today. I came right over there to see what the fuck was going on with her. She always went to work. I didn't understand why she was working in the first place. She pregnant and sick as shit most of the time, but she always went to work. I rushed my ass over there because for her not to go in, shit had to be all the way wrong. The door flew open, and some nigga was on the other side.

"What you need?" he asked.

I could see Z standing behind him pissed the fuck off. I looked at him then back at her.

"You good, Z?" I asked her.

"Nigga, don't ask her shit. I asked you what the fuck do you need. You're knocking on my baby mama's door and shit. What the fuck you want?" he asked.

"Oh shit. She ain't tell me her baby daddy was coming to town. I'm Zo, I live next door. I been kinda looking out for her and the baby since she moved in," I told him.

"You told this nigga you were pregnant? While you steady denying the shit to me. What the fuck, Z? You want this nigga to play daddy, I guess. You had no business moving ya ass down here, and you fucking knew you were pregnant. Slick ass mother-

WHEN THE PLUG HAS A THING FOR YOU

fucker. You really trying me with this bullshit. Are you fucking her?" he asked, looking back at me.

"Your ignorant ass really on one today. You need to stop acting like an asshole, Juma. I didn't tell him I was pregnant. He figured it out on his own. I just never told him different," Zinda tried to explain.

"Whoa. You ain't gotta come at me like that. I just told you I'm just looking out, that's all. She reminds me of my lil sisters, so I just help out when I can," I told him.

"She doesn't have a fucking brother, and she don't need one. Her hardheaded ass ain't have no business moving way fucking down here in the first place," dude yelled.

"You don't have to talk to her like that, yo," I said.

He walked up on me like he wanted to do something. I stood my ground, though. I didn't give a damn what kind of shit they had going on before, but he wasn't gonna talk to her like that in front of me.

"Juma! Juma! Will you stop? It's not that serious," Zinda pleaded.

"You got something to say to say to me, Craze Zo?" he asked me.

I didn't tell this nigga that my name was Craze Zo. I threw him the head nod to let him know that I understood where he was coming from. This nigga was on his shit. He knew who the fuck I was before I even said anything. I don't know who this nigga was, but he damn sure knew my ass.

"Zo, I'll call you later and explain everything. Let me talk to him first," Zinda said.

"You must be fucking this nigga or something. If y'all ain't fucking, you ain't gotta explain shit to this motherfucker. What the fuck you need to call him for? He's standing here right now, just say what you gotta say. I know all you gonna do is tell him that we not together no more like that means anything. I keep telling yo ass that we gonna get married. You're throwing a tantrum and moving down here just pushed the wedding date back. You ain't stopping shit with ya hard headed ass," he said.

We were nose to nose. He was talking to her, but looking me in the eye. I wasn't this nigga's competition, but if he wanted to get down and dirty, I was all for that shit. He stood in front of me biting his lip and shit. These up north niggas really thought they were putting some fear in our hearts with that silly shit they be doing.

"Will y'all stop? This is stupid. Juma, he's just a friend. It doesn't even matter. We are not together any damn way," Zinda fussed.

I could see her getting upset with tears running down her face. Looking at her made me want to walk away, but the man in me wasn't going no fucking where. This nigga was threatened by the wrong nigga.

"We together, yo ass just hardheaded. I just told you that. You deaf and pregnant now?" he said, still looking at me.

"I ain't the one you should be beefing with. You coming down here acting like this can't be good for her and the baby. Think about the shit you're doing," I told him.

Zinda came and forced her way between us. She was pushing her baby daddy and shit. I knew he was letting her ass push him though. If he wanted to do the damn thing, we could when she wasn't around because just like I told him, she's my sister, and that ain't changing. She pushed him in the house and shut the door.

I shook my head and took my ass to my apartment. I hit up my dude to see if he could find out who this nigga Juma was. He knew all about me, so why not return the favor?

I must have fallen asleep on the couch because there was a knock on the door. I got up to answer it, but was hit in the face as soon as the door opened. I didn't get a good look at who was at the door, but I stepped back and swung back at them. From there, it was on like Donkey Kong. Me and this nigga was going blow for blow. He was trying to get close to me to scoop me, but I wasn't letting that happen. That's when I saw that it was Zinda's baby daddy I was fighting. This nigga had to be fucking crazy.

"The fuck wrong with you, man?" I asked as we were tussling with each other.

"Stay the fuck away from my family," he said before swinging at me again.

"Fuck all that. I'm family, now what?" I asked him.

We both ducked when a gun shot went off. I looked up to see Zinda standing in the hallway with a glock in her hand.

"Get y'all dumb asses up. Juma, why you come over here fucking with him. I told you we only friends, but no, you had to bring your ass over here to fight. Then you wonder why I fucking left in the first place. You too fucking extra. Yes, I'm pregnant. Yes, it's yours. No, we not together. If you keep acting like this, we won't be anytime soon," she said.

The gun was moving all wild as her hand was moving around while she was talking. We were both ducking and shit, but she kept going on and on and swinging the gun around.

"Aye, put that shit down. Did you double check to see if the safety was still on?" I asked her.

"Fuck you, I know my way around a gun. If I wanted to shoot you two dumb motherfuckers, I would. You two gonna have to get y'all shit together. We not together, Juma, and I don't even look at Zo like that for you to be coming up here fighting the damn man. WE. ARE. JUST. FRIENDS. If this is what you came down here for, you can take your ass back to Virginia. You gonna fuck around and make me kill your ass," she said.

She took a couple of steps back, her eyes rolled to the back of her head, and she dropped to the floor.

"Zinda. Damn it Zinda can you hear me?" he asked.

He was over there just as she hit the floor. I grabbed my keys off the table.

"Scoop her up. I'll drive y'all to the hospital," I told him.

He scooped her ass up. and we headed out the door. We hopped in the car. He was in the back with her talking to her and trying to get her to wake up while I drove like a bat out of hell. Seeing her drop like that fucked my head up, so I knew he was going crazy.

When I pulled up to the emergency room, I threw the car in park. I opened the door for them to get out while I parked the car.

"Go 'head and take her in, I'll park," I said.

I jogged over to the car as I heard him yelling as they went into the building. I parked, but I had to smoke two blunts before

I went in the building. I hated fucking hospitals. I avoided them every chance I got. I knew I needed to be good and high when I walked back in there.

When I walked in, Juma was pacing back and forth. He looked scared as fuck.

"Did they tell ya anything yet?" I asked him.

"Nah, I'm trying not to go back there and see what the fuck is going on," he said.

I knew he was serious as fuck right now. He looked like he was stressed like a motherfucker. I admit, seeing her just drop like that made me feel some type of way.

"Aye, man. We good. I ain't mean to go off on you like that. She just drives my ass crazy," he told me, shaking his head.

"Real shit, I was trying to understand what took you so long to find her ass. I told her when she first got here that I knew whoever it was that knocked her up would come looking for her. I knew if I was you that I would hunt her ass down too. It's all good. Like I said, me and her don't rock like that. I knew when she got here that she was running from something. I wasn't gonna try to push up on her and get my feelings and shit all involved just to have you come whisper some shit in her ear and she be gone," I explained to him.

"I wish that shit was that easy. Her hard-headed ass gonna make me kidnap her ass. She knows damn well I would. After seeing her drop like that, she ain't gotta worry 'bout me getting her worked up. I ain't leaving unless it got something to do with business that can't nobody else take care of. I know you'll be there looking out for her, but other than that, she gonna get sick of my ass," he said.

I nodded my head in agreement because I knew where he was coming from. Women didn't understand that when a man loves, we love hard as fuck. I know it's a lot of guys out there that are dogs or male hoes, but that's because they been hurt or they don't wanna feel that kind of pain. The way Juma's face was right now, I hoped I never felt this kind of pain.

CHAPTER 9

JUMA

I know I needed to call Key to let her know what was going on with her sister, but I didn't have any answers yet my damn self. I held off on all that until I did. I didn't have time for Key and Sphynx to be arguing because of my phone call. We all know that they would probably end up shooting each other.

"How long y'all been together?" Zo asked me.

"According to me, a little over a year. Let her tell it, we were together for a few months," I answered.

"You know she loves you, right?" he asked.

"Why you say that?" I asked.

"Think about it. She's running from your ass because she's scared. Whatever you got her feeling is scaring her. She doesn't have control when it comes to you. She doesn't like it, so she's running. If you get her to stop running, y'all can be the next Jay and Beyonce," he told me.

I thought about what he was saying. Maybe the nigga was on to something. I couldn't worry about that now. I was 'bout ready to take my ass back there and find out what the fuck the problem was. I was back to pacing back and forth again. If I'm like this now, how the hell am I gonna be when she has the baby. I slid my hands in my pockets, trying to not look so nervous. I just couldn't sit still, though.

"Family of Zinda Martin," a chick said.

"Yeah, that's my wife, and this is her brother," I answered.

He looked at me with the side eye. I still had my eye on his ass because that fake brother/sister shit usually ended up with some fucking going on. For now, I would let them rock, though. I couldn't risk my lil man behind some bullshit. Trust and believe, as soon as they started moving funny, I was boxing both of their asses.

"She is stable. We are keeping her for two days for observation. She passed out due to her blood pressure being elevated. It's important that she stays away from stressful situations. We don't need her coming back here because her next step is bed rest for the duration of the pregnancy. She may need someone to stay with her as well to make sure she's taking care of herself.

"While examining her, there was a lot of scar tissue, so I would consider her a high-risk pregnancy. I put all the information in her chart so her OBGYN will be able to review those as well. We are having her put in a room. As soon as that is done, I will have one of the nurses come get you all so you can visit with her. Do you have any questions?" she asked.

"Nah, I just need to lay my eyes on her," I told her.

The other nigga just shook his head. I went to sit down. I was thinking about all the shit the doctor said. I got pissed because that meant I was gonna have to hold my fucking tongue about this shit.

"Yo, I just wanna let you know, if I find out you on that bullshit with Zinda, I'm gonna shoot ya ass quietly. I don't need her hearing the shot and going off on my ass. You say y'all tight or whatever in a brother sister type of way. Tell me what you know about this nigga at her job that's been slick stalking her?" I said.

Shit, he was talking about how he looked out, so he had to know 'bout the nigga.

"I don't trust his ass. He too fucking sneaky and shit. I had dropped her off at work a couple of times, and he was always asking fucking questions about who I was. I never said two words to his ass. He's trying too fucking hard, if you ask me. It's like he trying to get close to her for some reason. It's not that he just digging her either. The nigga reminds me of how a narc try to pop up on the scene and get in good with the crew. Then after they get in good, they kick the door in with them boys to take ya ass away," he said.

I nodded my head in understanding. I knew if he picked up on the shit then Zinda had to know something was up with the nigga. Hopefully, she kept shit basic with his ass. It's not like she didn't know the game or how to follow her instincts.

"Once she gets straight, I'm gonna leave. I know you staying here with her tonight. Just hit my phone if you need anything. You can call me too if you need a ride or some shit like that," he said.

This nigga might be alright, but I still didn't trust the brother/sister shit. Dick and pussy didn't give a damn who was on the other end. Long as they weren't blood relatives, they were fair game.

"Good looking out," I told him.

He gave me a head nod, probably thinking the same thing that I was thinking. *I gotta keep my eye on this nigga.*

The doctor finally came and got us. I stood in the doorway while ol' boy went in talk to Zinda. Her eyes were open, but I could tell that she was still out of it.

"You had my ass ready to fall out beside your ass. Don't do that shit no more. If you feel like you gonna pass out, just sit your ass down. You know shit got real when me and your baby daddy had to work together. You know that nigga don't like me. It's all good, though, because I wouldn't like my ass either if I was him. I just wanted to make sure you were up. I'm gonna head out. Looking at your ass pass out got me wanting to go by my mama's house to see my begging ass sisters." He laughed.

She gave his ass the middle finger. He gave her a head nod, and walked out the room. I stayed where I was. It just hit me that I'm gonna be somebody's daddy in real life. Not too long ago, I would have never even thought that I would be in a real relationship. That damn chocolate, bowlegged woman had changed all that shit for me. I was about to get emotional until I remembered she wasn't even gonna tell my ass that she was fucking pregnant.

"What the fuck did I do that was so bad that you didn't want me to know I knocked your ass up?" I asked her.

She rolled her eyes at me. No fucks were given; she had to give my ass some answers. Right now, was the best time to get them shits.

"I don't want to talk about this now," she said.

"Like I give a fuck. We're talking about it. We got a couple of days because you not going nowhere, and neither am I," I told her.

I walked into the room and closed the door. I pulled up a chair and sat in front of her. She tried to grab the remote to turn the TV on. I took that shit and yanked it so hard the cord that was used to keep it attached to the bed broke. I threw that shit across the room.

"What the fuck is your problem?" I asked her.

"Juma, just chill out. You here, I'm here, I'm still pregnant. You're winning," she said.

"Cut the bullshit. How the fuck am I winning? I had to bring my ass down here to find out you're pregnant? Why the fuck you act like you couldn't tell me you were pregnant, Zinda?" I asked her again.

"I didn't tell you because I didn't know if I was keeping the baby or not," she said.

I know I didn't hear her ass right.

"What you say?" I asked her.

I stood up from the chair I was sitting in. She looked at me all funny type. I wasn't gonna hit her ass or nothing. I just wanted to hear what she said better.

"I said I didn't know if I was gonna keep the baby," she repeated.

"Do you know now?" I asked.

"Yeah. I'm keeping the baby," she answered.

"So, why you ain't tell me when you figured that out?" I asked.

She was walking into this cussing out she was about to get. I was sick of her and her bullshit.

"I was going to call you," she said.

I sat back in my seat and looked at her. I wanted to choke the snot out of her right now.

"Let me get this right. Let me know if I'm wrong on anything that I'm about to say." I had to pause because I didn't want to yell, or throat punch her right now. "You're telling me that when you got here, you knew you were pregnant, but you didn't know if you were keeping it. Then, after you got here, you decided you were gonna keep it, but you still didn't tell me you were pregnant. You didn't even tell your sister. Now that I'm here, you really don't want me here, but you don't have a choice in that. So, what you trying to tell me is that if I make you mad or anything, you gonna kill my baby. You really don't want my baby, but you know if you kill my baby, I will most definitely kill you," I said.

I sat there looking at her to let that promise I just made sink in. I was dead ass serious too.

"Juma, you don't understand," she said.

"How can I understand anything when you spending all your time running from me instead of being a fucking woman and talking to me? You been walking around thinking that you couldn't get pregnant, but here you are. Instead of accepting the fucking gift that you have growing inside you, you had the audacity to even think about getting a fucking abortion. You gotta be the dumbest broad in the whole fucking solar system. Tell you what, after you have the baby, I'll take him with me. You won't have to worry about either of us. I'll stay here while you pregnant. I still got business to handle at home, so I'll be in and out, but I'll only leave for the important stuff.

"I'm done with you and this bullshit. You won't hear a word out of me about us being together or none of that. I love you more than I have ever loved any woman in my life, but if you don't understand that shit by now, I can't do nothing to show you anything different. You don't have to pay no bills, I'll take care of all that. Just don't flaunt no niggas in my face ,and I'll give you that same respect," I told her.

I got up and laid down on the hard ass couch in the room. Then I texted Sphynx and Key to let them know what was going on with Zinda. I know she was over there thinking it was some chick, but I wasn't gonna tell her ass no different. Did I believe the shit I just said? Fuck no. I was gonna cold shoulder her ass as much as I could. At the end of the day, she was gonna love the shit outta my ass. Just watch and see.

CHAPTER 10

SPHYNX

I was standing in the middle of the warehouse looking at one of the niggas that was caught on camera trying to steal some packs of pills from us. I didn't have no business being there, but with Juma out of town, I had to step in for the big shit. A nigga stealing was on my list of big shit.

"You still saying you ain't take the shit. We found it in your car. If you didn't take it, how the fuck did it get in your car?" I asked.

I was waiting on him to lie again. Nobody knew about the cameras in the house but me, Serion, and Juma. None of the lieutenants knew for this damn reason. If they knew, they would tell the workers. Whenever niggas thought the bosses weren't looking is when their true character comes out. This was why this nigga here was about to die.

"Fa real, Sphynx, it wasn't for me, man. My daughter is sick. She needs to have an operation and shit. I don't have the money, so I had to do what I had to do," he said.

Now this is where he dies. If the shit he said was true, I would probably hurt the nigga, so he can have a shit bag for the rest of his life. Knowing that this dumb ass didn't have any damn daughters pissed me off. The fact that he said the shit like that made me realize that this nigga didn't respect me or my intelligence. He really thought that shit was gonna change something.

TOY

"What's ya daughter's name?" I asked, fucking with him.

"Huh?" he said and looked up at me.

"Do you really think we had you working for us and we didn't know your family tree? You don't have a fucking daughter. Shit, truth be told, them boys you taking care of, only one of them came from your nut sack. You're taking care ya cousin's kids, with your dumb ass," I told him.

"Fuck you, nigga, you don't know shit. That's why y'all asses 'bout to die. Weak ass niggas," he yelled.

I turned and walked out of the warehouse. I walked past Lloyd, who was chilling by the door. He was the one we got to get rid of the bodies for us. He didn't talk much, but the nigga was in the loop about shit going on in the hood. He was loyal and stayed out of the spotlight, which is why I liked his ass.

"What you want me to do with him?" Lloyd asked.

"Closed casket. Hit me up when it's done," I told him before leaving out.

I got to the car, and the first thing I did was check my phone. I read the message from Juma and shook my head. This nigga was about to have me arguing with Key's short ass the rest of the fucking night.

I had seen all her fucking missed calls and voicemails. I knew when she read the text about her sister being in the hospital she would want to carry her ass down there with her. She should know me well enough to know that shit wasn't happening. She was too damn pregnant to try to save some damn body from they damn self.

The phone rang again with Key's name flashing across the screen. I kept on driving, remembering that I had to get gas, some blunts, and a six pack. I was in for a long fucking night, so I may as well get fucked up while Key's ass nags the fuck out of me.

I made my stop at the gas station and was pumping gas when I heard some tires screeching. I look up, and this fucking girl done brought her and my child up here to fucking argue. Which reminds me, I need to call Apple tomorrow and cuss they asses out for that damn Find my iPhone app. They needed to stop that shit from working for dumb ass crazy wives and girlfriends.

48

"I know you saw me calling and all the fucking messages I left. Why do you insist on making me act crazy?" she yelled as she walked up on me.

She knew damn well that I don't do acting out in public and shit. I tried to ignore her overly emotional ass.

"You need to take your ass home, man. Why the fuck you out here this late any fucking way?" I asked her.

"Nigga, my fucking sister needs me. I gotta go to Florida. I already brought my plane ticket. You wanna be out here running the street like we don't have a fucking family crisis going on," she fussed.

I walked over to her because I wasn't gonna do all this yelling and shit in public.

"Get your ass in the car and go the fuck home. You know I don't do all this rah-rah shit in public," I whispered in her ear.

I walked back to my car and glanced up to see her taking her pregnant ass back to her car. By the time we pulled up at the house, I had four beers left. I got out and went in the house behind her then closed the door and locked it behind me and set the alarm. I was not in the mood for this shit tonight.

When I walked into our bedroom she was sitting on the edge of the bed. Her leg was shaking fast as shit. I knew that meant she was mad, but she could stay that way all she wanted.

"Are you even concerned about my sister? She's fucking pregnant," she fussed.

I looked in the drawer for some boxers and a crisp white tee. I took my shoes off and put them in the closet. I then headed for the bathroom with her looking at me like I was crazy because I wasn't answering her. I looked down at her.

"Don't you fucking move. I'm going to hop in the shower."

She knew that I wasn't playing with her by the way I said it.

I took my shower, and when I came out, she was packing a suitcase. I stood there looking at her dumb ass. I just didn't understand where the fuck her mind was right now.

"You not going," I told her.

I wasn't yelling or anything. I was calm as fuck on the outside, but I knew that wasn't gonna last long.

"How the fuck you gonna tell me that I'm not going? I'm

fucking grown, just in case you forgot. I can come and go as I fucking please. My sister is down there by herself and pregnant. I can't leave her out there like that. She needs me," she argued.

See what I mean? I knew that calm shit wasn't gonna last long because just that quick I was in her dumb ass face.

"I. FUCKING. NEED. YOU. Did you forget that you are fucking pregnant too? Talking 'bout she down there alone. She chose to go down there. Didn't nobody make her do that shit. She's alone because she wanted to be. Let her rock with that shit.

"She knew she was knocked up when she left. She knew what she was getting into. So, why you feel like you gotta go down there to save her? She doesn't need to be saved. You tell me one more time that you feel like you grown, and Imma fuck you up. Being grown is not gonna mean nothing because if you take your ass to Florida, you gonna be dead and grown.

"You not even fucking thinking about OUR CHILD that's the crazy part. Do you need to be all fucking upset right now? Hell no. But you so busy trying to ride for your sister, and she not even concerned about your feelings or my child that you're carrying. The situation she's in is because of her fucking choices and nobody else's. Don't end up dead because of yours. I will fucking kill you if something happens to my son because you're running behind your selfish ass sister. Don't fucking test me because you will be in an adult size casket by this time next week," I told her.

I left her ass in the room. I was naked as hell. I had my clothes in my hand, but I had to leave her atmosphere. If I stayed in there with her, I was gonna do some shit to her that neither one of us needed. I knew she would be on one behind her sister, but there wasn't shit her ass could do about the shit. Zinda knew damn well she didn't have no business down there.

I went down to my man cave. After I put my clothes on, I turned the TV on and called Juma's ass up.

"Yo," he answered.

"I'm just checking on your ass. How's shit going down there? Oh yeah, that hole we had is clogged up too," I told him.

"Good looking out on that. As for shit around here, it's all fucked up. I told her she can be whatever she wanna be. I just wanna make sure my seed gets here alright. You know the fucked-up shit is that she don't see how fucked up her decisions are. She fucking told me that she didn't tell me about being pregnant because she didn't know if she was gonna keep it or not. You don't know how bad I wanted to choke her ass," he said.

I could hear he pain in his voice. She was fucked up for that shit, though. Zinda wasn't going to rest until Juma choked the shit out of her. He didn't hit females, but he damn sure would choke the shit out of them.

"I just had to threaten Mighty Mouse because she wanted to come down there," I told him.

"Nah, she doesn't need to do that. Zinda needs to learn from this bullshit. I told her I was gonna stick around, but I think I'm gonna leave and just come back when it's time for her to go to the doctor," Juma said.

"Man, you gonna leave her down there alone like that?' I asked.

I know he was pissed with her, but he couldn't leave her out there exposed. I didn't see how he could even think about leaving her.

"Nah, I'm gonna get somebody to come keep an eye on her. Her next-door neighbor said he would look out while I'm gone," he said.

"He? What the hell she got going on down there?" I asked.

"They say it ain't nothing. Me and the nigga had a nice little talk, so I know he'll look out for her," he said.

"Hey, if you like it, then I love it," I told him.

I shook my head because this shit was about to go left real soon. Ain't no way in hell I would leave Key down there like that. I didn't give a fuck if the nigga living next door was the fucking pope. As long as the pope had a dick, then the pope was suspect.

"Man, I'm just doing what I can do. I got a few days 'til she goes home. Once she gets settled at home, I'll be coming home. I think that's the best right now," he said.

"I'm with it. You go 'head and handle your business," I told him before ending the call.

I hoped this shit works out for his ass without any charges being filed.

CHAPTER 11

ZINDA

I was finally home in my own bed. I was surprised that Zo and Juma had been getting along with each other. I guess they needed to get that fight out of the way. Juma was hanging out with him and everything. Which was fine with me because he was straight curving my ass. He was only talking to me when he absolutely had to. The shit was weird as hell. I guess this is what life was gonna be like.

Tonight was the second night of me being home and they were gone to some bar. They made sure I was straight before they left, but I was feeling some type of way. Yes, I wanted them to get along, but they were being extra with it. They would come over together and sit there and talk to each other like I wasn't even there. I would just sit and listen to them talk about random shit. At the end of the night, they would go to their places and sleep, just to do the same shit again the next day.

I heard keys jiggling at my door. I knew it was Juma because Zo didn't have a key. Zo was cool and all that, but I didn't know him like that to have a key. The only reason Juma had a key was because his sneaky ass bought the fucking building.

I was on the couch with a tub of ice cream looking at old reruns of *The Golden Girls*. I didn't move when he walked in because I knew he wouldn't be there long.

"I just came to check on you before I went in the house. You good?" he asked.

"Yup," I said with an extra pop in the P.

"I'm going back home tomorrow night. I'll be back for all the appointments and shit like that. When I come for those, I'll stay for two days, then I'll be gone again," he said.

My heart started beating fast. I knew I said I didn't want him there, but I had gotten used to having him around just that quick. Now that he was giving me what I wanted, I didn't know if I wanted it anymore.

"What changed your mind?" I asked.

I was trying not to act too concerned, but I really was.

"I have some shit going on back home that I gotta handle. Hopefully, the shit will be done by the time you have the baby. If it is, I can stay here for a few months before I go back home. I'm not trying to be in your way either. You go back to work in a few days, so you'll be good," Juma told me.

"Oh, okay," was all I could say.

My mind was screaming for me to beg him to stay. My mouth stayed shut, though.

He got up and walked out the door. Once the door shut, I cried like it was the end of the world. This was my choice, so I had to deal with it.

∞∞∞∞∞∞

IT HAD BEEN TWO WEEKS SINCE JUMA LEFT. I KNEW HE HAD some eyes on me in addition to Zo. I had been back to work and was doing pretty good, but I was getting lonely and bored when I was at home. Most of the time I would call Key and talk, but lately that had been getting boring too. Sometimes Zo would come over, but he only came to make sure I had what I needed.

Juma's petty ass was only texting me once a day to make sure I was still pregnant. I told him before he put his petty boots on that I was going to have the baby. So, instead of answering his stupid ass question, I would just respond with the middle finger emoji.

"You look like you're deep in thought. Are you okay? You know if you wanna talk, we can. It doesn't matter what it's about," Kenny told me.

I just smiled and nodded my head. I didn't even remember him coming into the breakroom. I was in there minding my damn business, and here he comes. When I first started working there, he was an alright guy. Lately, he had been giving off a bad vibe. It was like he was trying extra hard to get close to me.

"I'm fine, just trying to get ready for the baby," I told him.

"Oh yeah. You never got around to telling me about your baby daddy. I know you said he was back home and all. It's just hard to believe that he hasn't even come down here to check on you," he pressed.

"I never said I was gonna tell you anything about him anyway. As long as I know who he is, that's all that fucking matters. Why you so aggy about him anyway? Do you know him or something?" I asked him.

"Pump ya brakes, lil' mama, I was just making conversation," he said.

"Well, you need to make conversation about something other than him. You're making me think you like niggas out here. Are you out here looking for some good wood too?" I asked him.

"Aye, that shit ain't funny," he said.

"I wasn't trying to be funny. Do you see me laughing?" I asked.

I wasn't trying to be funny, honestly. He was always bringing up my baby daddy. I was starting to think his ass was bisexual or something. Why was my baby daddy's existence bothering him so much? There was something going on, but as long as he didn't know anything, I didn't care.

"I'm not even gonna do this with you today. At first you were cool with us talking, and now you all hush mouth about stuff. I thought we were building a friendship," he said.

"We talk while we at work. How are we building a friendship if you and I only talk AT WORK? You don't know where I live. I don't know where you live. We don't talk to each other on the phone unless it's something work related. You starting to creep me out with how you're acting. You need to stay away from the Lifetime channel, seriously," I told him.

I walked out of the breakroom as fast as I could. I was getting a bad vibe from Kenny. I don't know what changed about him, but he was on his way to one of my bullets.

I worked the rest of my shift avoiding his ass like the Ebola virus. He was always looking at me every time I looked up.

When it was time for me to leave, I walked out of the building like it was on fire. He was calling my name, but I ignored him and drove out of the parking lot. On the ride home, I made up in my mind not to tell the boys about this because that would cause a lot of other problems that I didn't need. I would keep this shit to myself until he put his hands on me or made some kind of threat.

After I was home for a few hours, Zo came over to check on me before he went in the house. We chilled out for a little while.

"You sure you okay? You look like something on ya mind," Zo asked.

He'd been asking me that since he got there. I didn't know if he knew something or that he could just tell that something was on my mind.

"I'm fine, I just have a lot on my mind with the baby coming and all. I have a doctor's appointment next week, so Juma will be here plucking my nerves," I said.

"He just loves you and that baby you carrying. If it was me, shit would be totally different," Zo said and laughed.

"What you mean?" I asked.

I really didn't care, I just wanted to get my mind off what happened today at work.

"If you was my kid's mother, you would be sick of my ass. I would be all up under you. I wanna experience everything when my kids come. I wanna even try to eat all the nasty stuff that pregnant chicks be eating. My kids' mother is gonna breast feed too. Ain't no telling what's in that formula shit that they making now," he said.

"Well, I don't have that problem. He's back in Virginia doing God knows what," I said.

"You a damn trip, you know that? You miss that nigga, but

you too fucking proud to let him come help you out. You know you still love him. You haven't even given out your phone number. I know you pregnant and all, so you not fucking nobody, but you can still kick it with somebody," he said.

"I don't have time for that," I told him.

"Yeah, alright. That's why you be in here bored as fuck when you not at work. You can tell me the truth, I won't tell, I promise," he said with a smile on his face.

I threw one of the pillows from the couch at him. He was laughing all loud and shit.

"For real, you need to let go of whatever bullshit you're holding on to. That man loves the fuck outta you. You do know there's a thin line between love and hate, right? You need to get ya shit together, and that's coming from a nigga like me. You think niggas out here confessing their love and buying whole apartment buildings and shit just for anybody? Your ass betta wake up, Zinda," he told me seriously.

After both of us sat there quietly and wrapped in our own thoughts, Zo got up and left. I went to bed and cried myself to sleep again.

CHAPTER 12
JUMA

I was sitting in the back of another fucking strip club getting
drunk as fuck. Since I came back from Florida, I hadn't had
any type of sex. I was backed up and stressed the fuck out.
I hadn't been home in three fucking days. On top of Zinda's bullshit, somebody was fucking with me, and I had no clue who
it was.

When I say they were fucking with me, that's just what I
meant. At least one of my corner boys had been jumped every
fucking day. They wouldn't take nothing from them, just beat
they ass, tell them to tell me they were coming, and that's it.
They never said a name, just told them to say, 'I'm coming,' no
name, no nothing. The shit didn't make any sense.

Today, they took the shit to another level. Two of my houses
were kicked in. They beat everybody's ass in the house but left
the money and the dope. I was killing myself trying to figure out
who it could be. They always had on all black with a mask and
gloves.

I didn't have any family that I knew of. My grandma raised
me, but she was dead and gone. I was driving myself crazy. I had
been sitting outside all my spots as long as I could. I came to the
club to catch a nap and chill out before going back out to watch
my spots again.

The only smile that came across my face every day was when

Zinda would send me a middle finger after I texted her and asked was she still pregnant. I only did the shit to fuck with her.

"Man, you can't keep doing this shit. You need to go home and relax for a day," Sphynx said.

I forgot that nigga was with me tonight.

"Nah, if I go home, then I'm gonna be worried about shit going on out here. I would rather be out here when some shit pops off," I told him.

"You sure some of this ain't about Zinda?" he asked.

"It might be, but ain't shit I can do about how she feels. This street shit is something I can change, so I'm just focused on that right now," I told him.

He looked like he didn't believe me, but I was dead ass. I wasn't gonna press her about shit no more. She was the least of my worries. I needed to know who was out there beating up my folks. It was like they were watching me because they never hit while I was around. The shit just didn't make any sense.

"Heyyy fellas, is there anything I can do for y'all tonight?" a stripper came over and asked us.

I didn't even look up to see who it was. I just shook my head, telling her ass no.

"Really, Juma, that's how you carrying me right now? After everything that we been through?" she asked, getting loud.

I looked up to see that it was Cherry's ass. I didn't even recognize her voice before I looked up. I guess that showed how important she was to me.

"Walk away," I told her.

Just like I knew she would, she stood there ready to pop off with some more shit.

"Mother fucker don't act like you don't know me real well. Shit, if you would have let me ride that dick, you wouldn't be sitting over here like a bitch stole your heart. You too worried about her to see that your own team ain't fucking loyal," she said all loud and shit.

Tonight ain't the night for this shit. She got the right fucking one.

"You out here popping shit about my team like you know some real shit. What do you know, Cherry? Huh? I can't hear you," I said as I stood up.

TOY

"I'm just trying to show you that I'm loyal," she said.

I laughed in her face. Loyalty was not the first thing I thought of when her name came up or when I saw her.

"You loyal to a fucking nut. How you loyal, but you sucking off and fucking the whole damn crew? Ain't no loyalty in that," I told her.

"If you make me your number one, I can show you how loyal I am," she explained.

"Number one? What the fuck you on? You will NEVER be my number one. The only thing you can do for me is swallow a nut or three. I never went up in you raw because you out here busting it wide open for any nigga with a little money in his pocket," I told her.

"You gonna regret saying that shit to me," she said.

"Is that a threat? What the fuck you gonna do? You gonna suck me to death? You damn sure can't fuck me to death because your mouth is way tighter than your pussy," I told her.

She had the nerve to slap my ass. Hoes kill me. Just because I told her the brutal truth, she wanted to hit my ass. I walked up on her.

"Juma, she ain't worth it," Sphynx said.

She wanted a fucking scene, I was gonna give her ass one she would never forget.

"Get down on ya knees right quick. I'm trying to see something," I told her.

She looked at me like she was confused but got down her knees anyway. I started undoing my zipper.

"Juma, what the fuck you doing?" Sphynx asked.

"She threatening my ass. I wanna see if she can suck me to death in real life," I said.

He shook his head and she did what I told her to do. I slid my dick in her mouth. While she was trying to get in a rhythm, I took the bottle of vodka off the table. I took the top off. I could see her looking at me. That's another thing she did that I didn't like. Don't fucking look at me while you're topping me off. That shit is creepy as fuck.

"Don't stop. If you bite me, I'm gonna kill you," I told her.

Now everybody in our section had stopped enjoying themselves and were looking at me getting my dick sucked in front of everybody. Right before I came, I pulled out and shot my shit all in her face.

She wanted to say some smart shit so bad, but if she opened her mouth, my cum would have went in. I admit, it wasn't gonna be anything new to her, but I guess she didn't want everyone to know she swallowed. I was sure everyone already knew. I mean, she was cum catching Cherry.

When I was done cumming all in her face, I backed up to take a good look at her. Her face was covered with so much cum that it was dripping off her chin.

"You threaten me again, and I'll forget all about the excellent mouth game you got. If you ever approach me on some bullshit again, I will blow you and that bomb ass mouth piece you got away. If you not trying to suck my dick for the thrill of having a real nigga's dick on your tongue, act like you don't know me. If a bitch did steal my heart, she damn sure didn't do the shit on her knees. Get the fuck out my section, with your dumb ass," I told her.

I poured the rest of the vodka on her head. Now she was covered in vodka and cum, all because she didn't want to walk away.

"Your ass crazy as fuck, you know that? Why you do that girl like that?" Sphynx asked me.

"Fuck her and all these other hoes out here," I said.

I didn't have any love for none of them. Cherry should have known better than to try to act out in public. She must have forgot who the fuck I was. I bet now she remember that shit.

My phone rang, and I looked down to see that it was Zo. I picked it up quick as hell because I thought something was wrong with Zinda.

"What up?" I answered.

"Just wanna give you a heads up. She all in her feelings, and I think somethings going on. I just don't know what it is yet. When I find out, I'll let you know. Have you talked to her?" he asked.

"Nah, I been giving her the space she asked for," I told him.

"She lonely as fuck, but she not gonna tell you that. I'm

telling you, though. When I was over there earlier she looked like something was bothering her, but she never said what it was," he said.

"Good looking out, man, 'preciate this shit," I told him before ending the call.

I thought about calling her, but that thought only lasted for a little minute. She was tripping, so I was gonna let her keep on tripping 'til she fell down. I took my ass upstairs in one of the offices of the club to lay my ass down. I wasn't the owner or nothing, but I could still do shit like that just because of who I was.

I stretched out on the leather sofa after kicking my shoes off. I lay there for a few minutes before I just said fuck it. I dialed Zinda's number.

"Hello," she answered with a sniffle.

"Yo, you alright? You don't sound right," I said.

I sat up straight like I hadn't had a drink all night. I needed to make sure nothing serious was wrong with her or the baby. I never really heard her sound so fucked up and crying.

"I'll be alright. I wasn't expecting you to call, though. How are you doing?" she asked.

"I'm fine. You sure you don't need me to come down there early?" I asked.

"No, I'll be fine. I go through this sometimes," she said.

"Go through what, though? You still not telling me what's going on," I said.

"Nothing, really, I just get bored sometimes, that's all. There's nobody here with me. I know Zo is here, but he has a life, and he's so damn protective of me it's stupid. I think if I hit my toe on the nightstand, he'll throw the nightstand out." She giggled.

I was relieved to hear her laugh a little. I was jealous that she laughed because of him and not me, though. I know it's fucked up to think that way. I never wanted this shit, she did. So, if she was all fucked up because she was alone, there ain't shit I could do about it. I started thinking about the way shit was between us and got pissed all over again.

"Since you straight, I'm out," I told her before ending the call.

I knew if I stayed on the phone with her that my mouth would have fucked shit up even worse for us. I pulled out my phone and looked at the pictures and videos I had of her that she knew nothing about. I had pictures of her sleeping and random off-guard pics. I had a couple of videos of some of the conversations we had where she was laughing and playing around. I know it makes me look like a creep, but I'm not, real talk. I'm just a nigga in love like a motherfucker.

CHAPTER 13
CHERRY

Juma had embarrassed me for the last time. I rushed in the bathroom to clean my face off. I was so hurt that I couldn't stay in the club for the rest of the night. I walked out the door to see Polo and Draino standing outside. I didn't bother to acknowledge them. I just wanted to go home.

"Cherry!" Polo called out to me.

"Are you okay? I saw that bullshit go down. That shit was fucked up," he said.

"It wasn't fucked up enough for you to stop him, though. Miss me with all the fake concern you got for me. You just like the rest of these niggas out here," I told him.

I was pissed that Juma did me like that. I was more pissed at how much I still loved his disrespectful ass. I know now that he would never look at me as his woman.

"If you want, I can take you to get something to eat," Polo said.

"Nah, that's okay. I just wanna go home and think about some things," I told him.

"If you gonna think about getting back at that nigga, don't worry, I already got shit in motion," Polo said.

"Like what? He damn sure don't look like he hurting to me," I said and rolled my eyes.

WHEN THE PLUG HAS A THING FOR YOU

"Looks can be deceiving. I got my man to snatch some of his shit. The nigga fucked up and got caught, but he knew what he was in for," Polo said.

He was standing here like he had won the lottery or something. If he thought that little money he took was gonna do anything to hurt Juma, his ass was fucking clueless. Maybe I could use his ass to do what I needed him to do.

"Tell you what, we can go eat. I have some shit I want to run by you. I think we can help each other out in this," I told him.

While we ate, I told Polo what I thought we should do to drive Juma crazy. His product could be easily replaced, being that he was basically the fucking plug himself. I knew he was still copping from Serion. They were so close, I knew that Serion wouldn't let Juma take too big of a hit. We needed to hit him where it hurts. We needed to make his team fall apart from the inside out.

Once I explained everything I had in mind to Polo, he agreed that he would follow my lead. I told him he needed to recruit some more guys who would be willing to help with our plan. He said he would hit me up in a few days to let me know who was gonna be on our team.

Just when I thought this night was gonna end with me crying myself to sleep, it was actually gonna end with me feeling like shit was going to turn around for me. If my cousin, Kenny, was doing his part in making Zinda be a part of his life with or without her consent, my world was gonna turn out to be just how I wanted it after all.

"Since we gonna be running shit together, we might as well fuck to seal the deal," Polo said.

"Nah, little buddy. Ain't shit popping off with us until all this shit is done. Then we can fuck on Juma's money and over his dead body," I told him.

He just nodded his head, but I could tell he wasn't too happy. The thing about that is, I didn't give a fuck how he felt.

I had to call and make sure Kenny was doing what I needed him to do. I called him on my way home.

"Cuz, how are you and Zinda doing?" I asked when he picked up the phone.

"Man, she pissed with me. I was just trying to get her to see that her baby daddy wasn't shit but some street nigga. She got all protective of him. We got into a little spat, and now she's not talking to me," he said.

"You gonna take that shit lying down? You better make her understand that you're better for her than he is," I told him.

"Is her baby daddy there with her?" I asked.

I hadn't heard anything about Juma getting her pregnant, so it had to be a guy in Florida that knocked her up.

"Yeah," he said.

I rolled my eyes at how depressed he sounded. This nigga was looney. How can you be so broken up behind a bitch that's not even your friend?

"Well, go beat that nigga's ass and take your girl back," I told him.

"Okay, cuz, thanks," he said.

I ended the call and hoped he got this shit right.

CHAPTER 14
ZO

"You mean to fucking tell me that this nigga is the plug for most of the east coast? Am I reading this shit right?" I asked my man, Moe.

"If that's the nigga in that picture, then hell yeah. You were in the presence of fucking street royalty and didn't even know it. They say the nigga a little off, so look out for that shit," Moe told me.

I laughed because that nigga was more than just a little off. The nigga was ready to kill my ass, even though I was telling him I wasn't the one pushing up on Zinda. He didn't give a fuck, and still stole my ass. I could laugh at the shit now, but if Zinda wouldn't have come in with the gun, we would have killed each other.

"So, why you got me looking into a nigga from Virginia? You're fucking his girl?" Moe asked.

"Nah, nigga. Ol' girl next door is his baby moms," I told him.

"You are fucking his girl. Lying ass nigga," he said with a smile.

"I told your ass, me and her ain't like that. I wasn't even on that shit no more after I found out she was knocked up and hiding from that nigga. I'm glad I did the shit that way because even though we both told him nothing was going on, the nigga still fought my ass," I told him.

"Fuck you mean y'all fought?" he asked me.

"He knocked on my door and stole my ass when I opened it. It was on after that," I told him.

"You still alive, so why y'all stop fighting?" he asked.

"Why I gotta be the nigga to die? You supposed to be my nigga, and you gonna ask me some fucked up shit like that?" I asked him.

I wanted to steal this nigga's jaw. He was fucking out of line with that shit. I don't care if I was fighting Stone Cold Steve Austin, he betta have told my ass I won that shit. It didn't matter if I was being taken out of the ring in a fucking stretcher. When we get in the ambulance, he better dap my ass up and tell me I kicked his ass.

"My bad, nigga, damn. Why y'all stop fighting?" he asked.

"Ol' girl came over here shooting a gun and shit. When we heard the shot go off, we both stopped," I explained.

"Hold up, what's her name?" he asked.

"Zinda," I told him.

"She got a sister named Key?" he asked.

"I don't know. She got a sister, but she never said her name. Why?" I asked.

"Nigga! You're fucking slipping. Zinda and Key are some gangster ass sisters. They used to run with these niggas out of D.C. The two niggas are brothers too. One of 'em used to play baseball for the Nationals. He stopped playing after some personal shit went down. I think his wife or girlfriend got killed. He stopped playing and started taking over the streets," he said.

This nigga was all excited and shit like he was talking about a movie or something. I bet that nigga was ready to smoke or something the way he was all hype right now.

"Nigga, you alright ova there? You a little amped right now," I said, giving him the side eye.

"Fuck you, nigga. Getting back to ya girl, though. She and her sister don't mind a little gun play. They can box they ass off too. So, either situation, just know that she good. They were the cookers for the brothers at first, then they moved up, and now they treat them like their partners in whatever they do. They treat them girls like they blood. Her sister ended up with one of the brothers, I think. You done fell up on some real shit, nigga. If you don't make them kill you, this could be a fucking come up," Moe told me.

I hadn't even thought about a come up. I wasn't making chump change, but I wasn't a nigga that motherfuckers got excited when talking about me either. If that nigga connected like a plug should be, this could be a match made in heaven.

"The only thing is you better hope you don't fall in his girl's pussy. If you do, nigga, that's on you. But that pussy is for damn sure deadly. Proceed with caution like a motherfucker. You might want to just walk around wrapped in Saran Wrap while you around her," he said and laughing.

This nigga was falling out laughing at that dumb shit he just said.

"Don't look at me like that. Shit, if I was you, I wouldn't go around her without a vest on. You know how hormonal chicks are when they pregnant. She might kill your ass just because you and that nigga both got a dick," he said, laughing some more.

He was really enjoying himself.

"Get the fuck out, Moe," I told him.

"Hell nah. I'm coming with you to go check on ya so called sister. I need to see how you act around her to see if I gotta start making arrangements now." He laughed.

"Fuck you," I told him.

There was a knock on the door. I looked at him, and he started laughing harder. I opened the door, and it was Zinda. I could only shake my head at her timing.

"Hey, I don't mean to interrupt, but can you go to the sandwich place for me? I would go, but it's dark as fuck outside, and I don't feel like hearing Juma's mouth if something happens," she asked.

"You know I got you. You know what you want?" I asked.

"Yeah, I wrote it down," she said.

She put a piece of paper in my hand along with some money. I looked back to see if Moe was bringing his laughing ass. Of course, he was right behind me. We walked to my car, and I was almost in the car when she called my name. I looked up to see her coming to me.

"I might as well get two instead of one," she said with a smile.

She reached out to give me some more money.

"I got you, go back in the house before you get in trouble," I told her.

She laughed, but I was dead ass. I knew Juma had some niggas watching her. I didn't need that nigga asking me why she was outside with a fucking night shirt and some slippers on. I pulled off once she closed her door.

"Man, ain't no fucking way I would be able to keep my dick out of her. Bowlegged chicks are so fucking rare and sexy," Moe said.

"Guess I need to start making your arrangements," I told him and laughed.

He just shook his head, but I knew his ass was serious. I just wanted to be around when he tried his hand. I had to make sure to keep some popcorn around because that shit would be fucking entertaining.

CHAPTER 15
KENNY

Zinda was underestimating me if she thought just by her ignoring me was gonna make me go away. I had a job to do, and that is exactly what I was going to do. There was no way I could let her go now. I had pictures of her all around my house. She had her own wall filled with her pictures. There were pictures of us in the living room that reminded me of what we were before we got into it that day. I never wanted that one question to cause her to avoid me.

I got tired of waiting for her to answer my calls or talk to me at work, so I started following her. I knew where she lived, worked, and what grocery store she went to. I figured out that she chose to go to Target rather than Wal-Mart. Every day for the past week, I had been following her after work. I would follow her home just to sit in the parking lot until two or three in the morning. I would go home, sleep for a few hours, just to go to work and do it all over again.

I don't know when she changed from an assignment to a real-life goal for me. I had pictures of her that I had taken at work when she wasn't paying me any mind. Depending on what top she wore to work, her face would have this amazing glow. I know they said that pregnant women glow, but when she had on yellow, orange, blue, or pink, she could replace the sun in the sky.

She was too busy running behind that damn baby daddy of hers to pay me any mind. How can she be so wrapped up in a nigga who never had time to see about her or the baby? I only wanted to be the man for her that he obviously didn't want me to be. She deserved so much more. I could give her the world if she would only give me the time of day. I shouldn't have to see her smile from a distance.

Being a stalker was something I never thought I would become, but here I was sitting in the parking lot of her building wondering what she was in there doing.

I sat up straight when I saw some guys come out of her building. They were talking and laughing, but they stopped like someone had called them. She looked so beautiful. She was in her night clothes, obviously. Even with her head wrapped in a scarf and house shoes, she still made my dick hard. She talked to the guys for a few minutes, passed him something, and then went back into her place. He must be the fucking baby daddy.

I watched her baby daddy and his friend pull off. I was so pissed that I was squeezing the steering wheel so tight my fingers were hurting. I followed her from work and sat out there waiting to see who came to see her. I saw dude pull up hours ago. I didn't know that he was her dude, but seeing her come out dressed like that, he had to me. She had on this night shirt, but it wasn't as big as it needed to be. You could tell she had a banging ass shape under that night shirt.

I snapped a couple of pictures before following him. He stopped at a sub shop. I don't know what she saw in these thug type of niggas. He had tattoos everywhere, and shit, he looked like he had a gun on him somewhere.

I decided to go in the shop to see what this thug was really about. I walked in to see him sitting at one of the tables talking to his friend. I looked directly at him as I walked over to the counter to put my order in.

With each step, I got more and more upset. I hadn't talked to Zinda since the incident in the break room. It was like she forgot I existed, even though we see each other every day at work. She would look directly at me and not speak. She was ignoring my calls and not responding to my text messages like I had done something to her.

"You know me?" her baby daddy asked.

"No, but I think I seen you before. I think you fucking with my old side piece," I told him with a smirk.

"Nigga, how the fuck you sound? Who the fuck you talking about? You don't look like you know what to do with a main piece, talking about a side piece," he said.

"She ain't been here that long. She came from Virginia. I helped her get a job down here a couple of months ago," I told him.

"Names, nigga," he said.

I could tell he was waiting on me to say her name. He looked like he was getting upset by what I was saying, so I kept going.

"She got a weird as name to be a black chick. She nice, a chocolate, got them bowlegs that let you know the pussy good. That shit is fucking excellent. Pussy so good make you wanna move to another fucking country like Brazil or some shit, and still be faithful to her ass," I said.

"What's her name?" he asked.

He had stepped a little closer to me while his friend looked like he wanted to say something, but I cut him off. I was enjoying the confused look on his face.

"The shit start with a Z or an X," I said.

I started snapping my fingers like I was trying to remember. I could see steam coming from his head. My mission was almost accomplished, and now it was time for the final blow.

"Zinda, yeah, that's her name," I said.

I was about to start laughing, but I couldn't get the smile right because this nigga hit my ass. I wasn't expecting him to hit my ass. I stumbled back a few steps, only to be hit by his friend. I ended up on my hands and knees wondering what type of niggas these guys were. He didn't even say if she was his baby mama or not.

I guess I was right because these niggas were beating my ass. I tried to swing to hit one of them, but that didn't stop the blows from raining down on me.

"Hey, hey, stop it. You guys stop it. Take your food and go. Take your food and go," I heard someone say.

I silently prayed to God thanking him for the man who stopped me from getting killed. I was laying on the floor trying to move, but it seemed like I was paralyzed. I was lying on my stomach trying to get up. I couldn't see out of one of my eyes. There was blood on the floor, and one of my teeth was loose.

"Sir, sir, are you okay? Do you want me to call the police? You need to go to the hospital?" the owner said as he tried to help me up.

I pulled away from him just as I got to my feet.

"No, I don't need no help," I said.

I rushed out the door to get to my car. I had just touched the handle when I was hit again out of nowhere.

"You done fucked up, nigga. Never show your hand before you know what you're up against," the nigga said.

I couldn't see him, but it was the same voice of Zinda's baby daddy. I couldn't just let him sit there and fuck me up like this, especially after I'm the one who started everything.

"Fuck you, that's why ya girl a fucking hoe out here in these streets," I told him.

"You's a dumb ass mother fucker," he said.

I felt something else hit me before I blacked out right in the parking lot.

CHAPTER 16

ZO

I was fucking thirty-eight hot when I got to the car. I figured out that the nigga was that Kenny motherfucker from her job. I know I was using fuck and motherfucker a lot, but that's just because I'm pissed the fuck off. I was ready to go back to the store, wake his ass up, and knock him out again.

"I got the food, man. I know your lil sis was gonna fight your ass if you didn't come back with her food. She would fuck your wanna be Apollo Creed ass up," Moe said.

"'Preciate it," was all I could say.

How do you walk up on somebody and just start talking shit? I mean, he straight running his mouth like he knew what the fuck he was talking about. Just wrong and fucking loud. The shit started bothering me that he even approached me. I knew he had to have been following Zinda because we weren't out in public together that much.

The more I thought about it, the more the shit didn't feel right. I pulled out my phone and hit up Juma. He needed to bring his ass down here because some bullshit was going on that we knew nothing about.

"Yo," he answered.

"Aye, did your boys that you have on Zinda say anything about her being followed?" I asked him.

"Nah. Why? What's going on?" he asked.

"I just got approached by that nigga Kenny that she works with," I said.

"Da fuck you mean approached?" he asked, cutting me off.

"He came up on me talking shit about how I was fucking with his old bitch. The thing is, he said she was his side piece. Trying to make it look like she some type of hoe ass thot out here. The trip shit is he thought I was her baby daddy," I told him.

"Oh, hell nah. Why would he approach you, though?" he asked.

"That's why I asked had yo people said anything about her being followed. It can't be a coincidence that I'm at the place getting her one of those nasty ass sandwiches, and he walks up on me. I just left the damn apartment building and came straight here. That means he had to be watching her ass. Where yo people at?" I asked.

"When you get back to the spot, kill them niggas. They in a silver Impala. Ain't no fucking way they there and some nigga following her ass. How could they not see the shit? I'm flying out first thing in the morning. I got some shit going on, but my family is more important. Good looking out on the call. Don't tell her ass shit. I'll talk to her tomorrow when I get there. Just tell her you ran into some niggas you got beef with or some shit. She doesn't need this shit on her mind right now," Juma told me.

"Indeed. I'll take care of that for you. Hit me up when you touch down," I said.

"Cool," he said before ending the call.

"What he say?" Moe asked.

"He wants me to kill the niggas he brought down here to follow her," I told him.

He gave me a funny look.

I just nodded my head because I knew what he was thinking.

"Yeah, he said it on the phone in those words," I told Moe.

He just chuckled. It was a street rule not to discuss shit like that over the phone. If you did, you were supposed to speak in code or use different words just in case them boys was listening.

"He just doesn't give a fuck if them boys was listening, huh? Shit, maybe he knows some shit we don't know. I know he has some of everybody in his pocket from street cops to judges, but damn. He's bold as hell with it," Moe said.

We pulled up to the apartment complex. I scanned the parking lot to see if the Impala was in the area. It was parked way back in the corner. I almost missed the shit. From where they were parked, I knew they didn't have a clear line of sight of Zinda's apartment. No wonder these niggas didn't know about anybody following her. They didn't know what the fuck they were doing.

"You need me to handle that for you?" Moe asked.

"Nah, I got it. Hold tight, I'll be right back," I told him.

I walked over to the parked car. I could see as I got closer to the car that one nigga was into his phone and the other one was sleep. I was hoping for the nigga in his phone to at least look up. I shook my head as I stood by the door, and he still hadn't looked up. Then, on top of that, this nigga was playing Candy Crush.

I finally tapped on the window with the barrel of the gun. I signaled for him to roll the window down when he looked up.

"Did y'all see any cars following Zinda?" I asked.

"Nah, we ain't see nobody," he answered.

I know I didn't have to ask, but I did anyway because I just wanted to see what they had to say. Moe was talking about how Juma was a real nigga, but his choice of niggas to watch his family was wrong as fuck.

My phone started ringing. I saw that it was Juma, so I answered it.

"Yeah," I answered.

"Did you kill them niggas yet?" he asked.

"Nah, I'm standing here now. What's up?" I asked.

"Ask them if they moms still stay in the same house," he said.

"Yo, Juma wanna know if y'all moms still stay in the same house," I said.

"Yeah," he answered.

"Okay, cool. Let me hear it," Juma said.

I shot the nigga I was talking to in the side of his head. When the shot went off, the sleeping guy woke up trying to figure out what was going on. I shot him in his forehead when he looked at me. I slid the gun back in the back of my jeans.

"Thanks, man, 'preciate that shit," he told me.

"No problem. I got a question, tho. Those niggas was brothers?" I asked.

"Yeah, twins. It's fucked up that they mom lost her last two sons tonight, but they fucked up. Then they fucked up and started playing with my heart. That shit can't slide. I'll make sure they mom straight though. Good looking out on calling me 'bout that nigga. It's obvious as fuck that they didn't know what the fuck they were doing," Juma argued.

I knew he was pissed because I could hear it all in his voice. I also knew that this was my opportunity to show him what us Florida niggas were about.

"I'm gonna call some of my boys to watch her. I'll handle that on this end so you won't have to kill any more of your crew," I said with a laugh.

"Sounds good to me. I forgot to ask did you beat that nigga to death?" Juma asked.

"No, he was sleep in the parking lot when I left. I doubt he dead. He might wish he was," I told him.

"Do you know anything about him?" Juma asked.

"His name is Kenny. He's been at his job for almost ten years. He been sniffing around Zinda since she got here. Real shit, I think he wants to be her man and her baby daddy. He seemed a little off when he was talking to me. Something about him let me know that he is definitely gonna be a problem," I told him.

"I guess that's a problem I'm gonna have to take care of personally," he said.

"If you need me, just let me know," I told him.

"I might need you, but we can discuss that when I get there," he said before ending the call.

I slid the phone in my pocket and started back to the car. I had stopped walking while I was on the phone. Moe saw me coming and got out of the car.

We took Zinda her food. She was complaining about us taking so long, but I knew that was gonna happen. When we got back in my place, that's when Moe started with the questions.

"What that nigga say? I know he was who you were talking to," he said.

"Calm your groupie ass down. He said he needs me to do something, but we gonna talk about it when he gets here," I told him.

"Oh shit. Nigga, this our come up. I bet money on that shit," Moe said excitedly.

I shook my head at his thirsty ass. Moe was always looking for a come up. Don't get me wrong, he wasn't a grimy nigga, he just was a hungry nigga.

I shot the cleanup guy a text, so he could come get those niggas' bodies. I should have done it right after I did it, but them niggas weren't going anywhere. I took my shower and kicked back in my room until I went to sleep thinking about what Juma could be asking me to do.

CHAPTER 17

ZINDA

The other night something seemed off with Zo when he brought me my food. His mood seemed different from the one he had when he left to get the food.

I got up early this morning to clean house while I had some type of energy. I had R. Kelly playing as I cleaned the house. Music always helped me clean faster. Without it, I would find other shit to do before finishing.

Today, I planned to go get some furniture for the baby's room. I was technically only three months, but it was better for me to get this stuff set up now before I got to looking like a whale. I decided to just get the furniture, but not the clothes or sheets yet. I was saving that for when I found out what I was having.

I knew I couldn't depend on Juma to be here to help because he was traveling between here and Virginia.

I heard my front door open, but Juma wasn't supposed to be there yet. I knew he was coming for my appointment, but that wasn't until next week. I slowly crept down the hallway with the broom in my hand, ready to crack a nigga's head open with it.

"Juma! What the hell are you doing here? Why didn't you call me to tell me you were coming? I could have had company here," I told him.

He gave me a damn smirk, tossed his keys on the table, and

went to the bathroom. I stood there trying to digest the fact that he completely ignored me. When he came out, I was standing in the same spot.

"Why you still holding the broom like you gonna hit me? I came early because I wanted to chill for a couple of days before going back after the doctor's appointment," he said.

I looked at him for a few, trying to decide if I wanted to press the issue more behind this pop up. He was serving me bullshit on a china plate right now.

"You can't run shit in Virginia coming here all the time. Like I said, you just can't pop up like that because I could have company here. A simple phone call would be the right thing to do," I told him.

"Okay, look, you not having company. Not no male company anyway. As for me popping up, I'm gonna keep doing it. You're walking around with a piece of me inside you. I will come and go as I fucking please. Talking about a fucking phone call. Yeah, alright, a damn phone call would have been cool too before you brought your retarded ass down here. If you never ran down here, I wouldn't be going from here to Virginia all the fucking time. I can run shit from wherever I want to. I don't need to be there for them niggas to know not to fuck up. You should know that shit," he told me.

I kissed my teeth and headed back into the room that was going to be my baby's. He followed behind me.

"Why you using all these stinking ass chemicals? You gonna have my child come out all fucked up because you using all this shit. It can't be good for the baby," he said.

"Don't you have a place upstairs that you need to be in?" I asked him.

"No, but I have a pussy that I need to be in, but your ass being all selfish," he said.

"Why are you here?" I asked him.

"I told you why I'm here."

"No, you tried to feed me some bullshit," I told him.

"Real shit, I'm just here to spend some time with you. You know just us two friends. I know we not together, so don't tell me again. All I'm saying is that we need to learn how to get along before the baby gets here," he said.

See what I mean? He still playing, telling me that shit. I dropped it. The real reason will come out sooner or later. He could say whatever he wanted, but I knew something was up. First, Zo is acting weird, now Juma is here way early for my doctor's appointment. I just hope when it does come out, I don't have to kill his ass.

∞∞∞∞∞∞

ME AND JUMA HAD BEEN GOING BACK AND FORTH FOR THE past couple of days. Now it was time for me to go to work. I took a few days off just because I hadn't been feeling too good. I was happy as hell that I only threw up twice today. Usually, I'm throwing up all over the place in the morning.

The ride to work wasn't bad either. Maybe today is going to be a good day.

I got to work on time, so I headed to my desk. I saw a group of employees huddled up in the corner. That's that shit I hate about working there. They had all these fucked up cliques. Everyone in the huddle was messy as fuck, so I knew it had to be something juicy that they were talking about. I didn't stop to find out what the latest rumor was.

"Zinda, did you hear about Kenny?" Alicia, one of the workers asked.

"No, what happened? Did he get a promotion?" I asked her.

Alicia was the queen of messy and drama. She never talked to me. We speak when we see each other, but never have a conversation.

"Girl, he in the hospital. According to Sam, he isn't doing good at all," she said.

"What happened?" I asked her again.

"He got jumped by six white guys. Both of his eyes are swollen shut," she shared with me.

I felt bad when she said that. I knew me and Kenny hardly ever saw eye to eye about anything, but I don't want to see him get hurt. The way Alicia was smiling, I could tell that she didn't care for real. It was a damn shame how people around there were only worried about people when shit got bad. This whole time, I had never seen her say shit to Kenny. Now since he got hurt and she has something to talk about, she got his name all in her mouth. I was still setting up my desk when I noticed that she was still standing here.

"What's the matter? What else do you need to say?" I asked.

"Nothing, he's at Westchester General Hospital if you want to go check on him. My sister is one of the nurses in the emergency department. She told me he was brought in," she said.

"I'll just sign the company get well card that they're gonna send," I told her.

I knew damn well I wasn't signing the card either.

She was still fucking standing here.

"Why the fuck you still standing here? What you got to say?" I asked her.

"I heard that he got in an argument with your baby daddy. I didn't know you liked vanilla like that," she said.

"So, your sister told you all of that? If she's a nurse, how she know all that?" I asked her.

I despised all her gossiping and extra shit that she constantly did. It was funny as hell to me because Juma was the furthest from a white boy.

"Well, the owner of the store that he got beat up in came in while he was getting worked on. He was telling the police what happened. Your name came up, and the words baby daddy came up. It doesn't take much to put two and two together," she said.

"If your sister is a nurse, why is she eavesdropping on other folks' conversations? I'm sure there was a bed pan that she could have been cleaning or something," I told her.

These people around here, man, I tell ya. Everybody was so fucking concerned about my baby daddy. Why the hell are they so pressed about him?

"When did you say this happened?" I asked her.

"Two or three nights ago. As a matter of fact, it was the night of the last time you worked. Funny how that worked out. You haven't been to work, and he been in the hospital. Are you sure you don't know nothing about it?" she said.

"Well, that would be impossible. He lives out of town, and he wasn't here that night. I don't even know why I'm talking to your ass. All you do is walk around here acting like you run this shit. All you run is your mouth. You need to keep my name out of your mouth. Next time you say some shit about me and mine, me and my baby are going to kick your ass. Get away from my desk, and have a fucking productive day," I told her.

I wasn't trying to fight this hoe, but if she kept on, I was going to throat punch her ass. I came down there to start fresh without all this extra shit. Yet, here the fuck we are.

I hit Juma up to see what the fuck was going on. I knew something was up with him just popping up on me. Depending on what I found out, the new Zinda was getting put on the shelf for a little bit.

CHAPTER 18

JUMA

I was riding with Zo and his man, Moe. We were on our way to meet up with some niggas that he trusted. I was about to offer this nigga the come up of a fucking lifetime. I needed him to take me up on this shit. I had already talked everything over with Sphynx and Serion, so they knew what was going on, and they were on board.

My damn phone started ringing with Zinda's name flashing.

"Yo," I answered it.

"A guy at my job got beat up pretty bad a few nights ago, and they saying you did it?" she asked.

"You sound dumb as hell right now. How the hell am I gonna beat some nigga ass all the way from Virginia? I can't believe you even called me about this bullshit. If it just happened a few days ago, how the fuck they know the details?" I asked her.

"Juma, do you know anything about this? Because it's weird that they saying you did it out of everybody in the world?"

"I just got here the other day. I been in your face the whole time, so when could I have beat your friend up? I'm trying to handle some shit, but here I am on the phone going back and forth with you about this shit," I told her.

"Don't let me find out you had something to do with this shit. I'm fucking you up if you did," she threatened.

"Can you just fuck me instead? It's been a minute since I got some ass. You better be glad you already pregnant because I promise if I go up in you it's certified that you gonna get knocked up. Tell me I can slide up in it, and I'll tell you I killed JFK. My black ass wasn't even born then, but for a piece of you, I'll confess to that shit," I told her.

"Dumb ass," she said before ending the call.

"I know who that was," Zo said.

"She pissed that people at her job talking about I beat ol' boy ass," I told him.

"How they know that? Nobody else was in the shop last night. I guess his ass told somebody. Guess that nigga ain't dead because dead niggas don't talk," Zo told me.

"He not dead yet," I told him.

That nigga was gonna have to go. I just needed to find out what his end game is first. There has to be something else going on. We pulled up at the meeting spot. There weren't many people there, but I did tell him to call the niggas that he would trust with his child's life.

"What's up, fellas? This is Juma. You may or may not know the name. He has an offer to put on the table. The only reason why y'all are here is because he told me to call the ones that I would trust with my child's life. So, pat yourselves on the back. Y'all made the cut. Now, if you down with what he says, then stay. If not, carry yo ass, but don't repeat shit you hear in here today," Zo told them.

"Imma get to the point. I need some new faces to come back to Virginia with me. I got some whodini motherfucker trying to sabotage my shit. The only way I can find out who it is if I get some new faces to act like they trying to get put on. I need them to act like I won't put them on, and they pissed about it. That way, whoever it is will think they have an advantage.

"I don't know who the person is, but I know how a boss moves. If this cat is a boss, he's gonna try to get you to get down with my crew. The problem with Virginia is that everybody knows everybody. If you a new face, you don't have alliances with anyone in the area. You can act like you all for what this dude has going on. I don't need to know the plan that they have for me. I just need to know who the fuck it is.

"If you help me with this, I will start supplying y'all with my pure shit for a fifty percent discount. The discount will be for the next two years, then after that, it goes to regular price. This is a win-win situation. Y'all get put on with the pure shit, I get to cut the head off a roach that won't die, and we all make fucking money," I told them.

I looked around the room and waited to see if anyone would leave. No one did. Not one nigga in the room looked like he was nervous about anything I said. If these niggas are as thorough as they seem, shit was about to get real.

CHAPTER 19
KENNY

I could see the bright light above me through the little slit in the swelling of one of my eyes. I could barely see enough to make out any faces, but the light, I could definitely see. I started feeling around, and I could tell by the smell and the rails on the side of the bed that I was in the hospital. I just didn't know how long I had been there.

"Sir, nice to see you are awake. Let me get your vitals, then I will go get the doctor," the nurse said.

I was starting to panic because I didn't know where I was or how long I had been there. I remembered the fight, but after that, I only remember walking out of the sub shop. The more I tried to remember, the more my head started to pound with pain. I tried to lift my hand, but I couldn't because of all the shit they had me hooked up to.

"Hello, sir. I'm Doctor Tolbert. It's nice to see that you've come back to us. We were scared for a minute there. Well, getting to the point of how you ended up here. You were assaulted a few days ago. You have been in and out since you got here," the lady doctor told me.

She poked me and asked me some questions about how I was feeling before leaving me in the room alone. I lay there wondering what I could do to help Zinda see that her baby daddy was nothing but some street thug. He couldn't give her a promising future like I could. I was gonna call her later on, so we could finally talk about things and start building our foundation.

I waited until it was almost nine o'clock before I dialed her number from the hospital phone. I was hoping that she would answer the phone for a number she didn't know.

"Hello," she answered.

"Zinda, how are you? I'm just calling to check on you," I said.

"Kenny? Is that you? Where are you calling me from? I heard you got beat up. Why are you calling me?" she asked.

She was concerned about my wellbeing. That alone made me smile. I knew she was just acting like that because we were at work.

"I'm calling because you were on my mind. I got into it with your baby daddy. I admit I said some shit that could have pissed him off, but..." I said.

"What are you talking about? My baby daddy just got here a few days ago. I think he got here after you were already in the hospital," she said, cutting me off.

"No, that couldn't be right. We got in a fight at the sub shop," I told her.

"Sub shop? He was with another guy that night, right?" she asked.

She sounded like she was going to say something else. I waited few moments, but she never said anything else.

"Yeah, they jumped me, I think. I still can't remember everything, but he was the guy I was talking to at first," I told her.

"I'm sorry for that. I don't know what all of that was about, but I'll find out. You just make sure you get your rest and get better," she told me.

I wanted to stay on the phone with her longer, but I didn't want to press my luck. I was just enjoying the sound of her voice for however long I could. That's all I wanted was to hear her sweet voice every day. I got that, so I was good until I could see her. Just thinking about her made my dick get hard. Here I am in the hospital, and all I can think about is fucking her. This chick was gonna be the death of me.

CHAPTER 20
ZINDA

After ending the call with Kenny, I sat on the couch waiting for Juma to bring his ass through the door. Kenny had just confirmed that he had gotten beaten up by Zo and not Juma. I never confirmed or denied if Kenny was fighting my baby daddy or not. With Zo being the one Kenny was fighting, I knew for sure that Juma knew about it. I just didn't understand why it had to go like that.

I heard the keys in the door, so I turned the TV off and sat back so my face would be the first thing he saw.

"Sup?" he asked when he came in.

"I thought you told me you didn't have anything to do with Kenny getting beat up?" I asked him.

He locked the door and sat down on the sofa next to me.

"Okay, and? Why are you asking me about this shit again?" he asked.

"I'm asking because he called me. I just got off the phone with him not too long ago, and—" I was explaining before he started talking.

"Man, you not gonna sit here and question me about some shit that bitch ass nigga told you. I found out about the fight after the fucking fact. I wasn't trying to take shit there with you because of your dumb ass falling out the last time you got all worked up. I see looking out for you ain't something that you appreciate, so I'm not gonna do the shit no more. You wanna know what happened. I'll tell your potato head ass. That nigga that you was just kee-keeing with on the fucking phone been following your ass," he said.

I looked up at him with a confused expression. I never noticed anyone following me before that day.

"Nah, don't look like that now. Don't fucking say nothing either 'til I'm finished. That nigga wants you. He wants to fuck you so bad that he's been following your ass. He on some type of stalker shit with your dumb ass. He approached Zo talking about how you were his ex and how good your pussy is. Zo got tired of him being disrespectful to you, so he rocked his ass. Did he tell you that part?" he asked.

I couldn't respond because I was still thinking about him saying Kenny had been following me.

He shook his head and stood up.

"Fuck this shit, man. You gonna fuck around and have me co-parenting with your ass for real. I'm doing everything I can do to keep you safe, and you steady listening to everybody but me. I'm the motherfucker that loves you, and you straight being a weak ass bitch right now. When you look up and I'm not trying no more, don't go around town telling everybody that I ain't no good. Tell them the truth; that I'm too good for you," he said.

He wasn't yelling at me, but his words along with the look in his eyes caused me to start crying.

"Hell nah, you don't get to fucking cry your way out of this. That nigga could have snatched you up or worse, but you straight taking his word about shit. I never gave a fuck about what other people thought about me, but you ... your ass is different. I've done way more than I should have for you. It's been that way since I met your black ass. Not no more, though. Fuck it and fuck this. I got too much shit back home going on to be worried about you just because you too fucking weak and scared to be with me. Don't try to make a damn scene when you see me with somebody else. I promise you I will embarrass the fuck out of you. We don't have shit else to talk about," he said.

"Juma, we have to talk. We have a baby together," I told him.

"Nah, just go back to your original plan. Do all this shit by yourself. You remember when you were running around making decisions without me like my nut didn't make the baby you're carrying. You did all that by yourself, right? You're a bad bitch, right?" he said.

I knew he was trying to be funny, but that was not the time.

"Don't you leave without us agreeing to something, Juma. We have to think about our future," I told him.

"Agree? Agree? Bitch you must've bumped your damn head. Fuck agreeing. You not concerned about me or my fucking feelings. When he kills your ass, I'm not coming to the funeral. You so fucking hard headed you probably thinking that there's a logical reason for him to be following your dumb ass. You wanna know what the reason is? The reason is because even though you can fight, cook dope, shoot guns, and smuggle shit, you still a silly ass bitch at the end of the day. You gonna go for whatever he tells you, even though you know me better than anybody. You should know that I'm over this bullshit with you. I wasted all this fucking time chasing your ass for nothing," he said.

He walked out the door, slamming back shut.

I sat on the couch and cried.

CHAPTER 21
KEY

My ringing cell phone broke my damn sleep. I just fell asleep not too long ago. Sphynx was still giving my ass the cold shoulder, so he was in the guest bedroom.

"Hello," I answered.

"Key, he's gonna leave me to raise this baby alone. I don't know how to do it on my own," Zinda cried.

I sat up in my bed and rolled my eyes. She was plucking my damn nerves already. If she kept on with this mess, tonight would be the night that I told her that shit.

"What happened?" I asked her.

I didn't really want to hear it, but I knew she needed to get some stuff off her chest. I was gonna let her explain herself. She babbled on for about fifteen minutes before she stopped talking. She was crying so bad that I knew she was looking real ugly right now.

"What should I do?" she asked me.

"You need to boss the fuck up," I told her.

She got quiet, which I knew she was gonna do. It never fails, she always wants to get quiet when she knows she's the one in the wrong. Right now, she was wrong as fuck. I should have broken this shit down for her before she left. I was done being nice to her and she's acting like a dumb blonde.

"Key, I don't know if," she said.

"How can you know if you never try? Juma loves your ass, and you too damn stupid to realize it. He been chasing after your ass, but you still running. You don't care about anybody else but you. Not Juma, and not me. Do you know your bullshit is fucking up my household? Sphynx is so pissed with me about not telling him about you leaving or being pregnant that he barely talks to me. We're sleeping in separate rooms, and that's only when he's not in the street. On top of that, they have somebody out here at Juma's fucking head.

"Did you hear me? THERE IS SOMEBODY OUT HERE TRYING TO KILL THE MAN THAT LOVES YOU! You so busy out here wrapped up in the fake ass problems in your head that you gonna look up and that nigga gonna be in a casket. If you get in his funeral and start acting a damn fool, I'm gonna fuck you up my damn self.

"You need to stop adding stress to his life. You are supposed to be his peace not another war. If y'all don't get together, you can't blame anybody but your own ass. You can fuck up a wet dream with your bullshit. I still don't know what the fucking point was of you going all the way down there," I said to her.

"Wait a minute what you talking about somebody is after him?" she asked.

"Somebody's been kicking in the traps and beating up his corner boys. Every time, they leave a message for Juma. You playing games and we dealing with real life 'round these parts," I told her.

"I love him. I just, I just," she said.

"You just acting like a confused ass bitch for no reason. If you love that nigga, let him know. As far as I'm concerned, he's proven his love for you. You're the one that's suspect. You're my sister, and I love you to death, but I wanna slap the shit out of you. Why the hell did you leave in the first place?"

"I left because I didn't know if I could be the wife and mother that everyone expects me to be. I felt like he can do better," she said.

I swear she was my sister by blood, but her fucking common sense was non-existent.

"I call bullshit. People have doubts all the time, but they don't leave the fucking state because of them. You need to get your shit together," I told her.

"I will, I promise I'll make everything right again."

"You need to because your bullshit is fucking up my dick diet," I said.

She giggled a little bit, but I was fucking serious. Sphynx hadn't touched my ass since all this shit had been going on. Here I am pregnant and horny just as much as my eye lids blink. I knew I was at risk for carpal tunnel and catching a charley horse in my hands by now. I was starting to get a headache, so I ended the call.

"'Bout time somebody cussed her spoiled ass out," Sphynx said from behind me.

I didn't even know he was back there. I was too pissed to even deal with his bullshit tonight, so I didn't respond to him. I eased down inside the covers to get comfy and go back to sleep. If I couldn't ride my husband's dick in real life, I could at least do the shit in my dreams. If I wasn't so damn tired all the time, I would rape his ass.

I felt the cold air as he got in the bed behind me. His arms wrapped around me. Feeling his big hands palm my belly, I prayed silently that tonight I was gonna be blessed with the good wood.

"I miss you, Key," he whispered in my ear.

I moaned as I felt him kiss my neck. My eyes closed on their own. I think I was about to cum just from him touching me. I hoped this was the prelude to some dick because if it's not, I was gonna fight this nigga tonight.

"Thanks for setting your sister straight. That's all I wanted you to do. Stand up for what's right. Stand up for us. No one should ever come before us. Don't allow outside shit to cause problems in your house. Your loyalty is to God, Me, and our family. All that other shit doesn't count. Open them legs so I can feel my wife again," he said.

I did what the hell he told me to.

CHAPTER 22

ZINDA

All night, I thought about what Juma and Key told me. I was being dumb coming all the way down there. All I had to do was talk to him about how I felt. Now, here I was sinking lower and lower. I needed to get it together for this baby and for the man who held my heart. The first thing I needed to do was go talk to Kenny and see what was going on with him.

I got up, handled my hygiene, and went to start putting my life back together. The ride there I was trying to gather in my head what I wanted to say to him. When I got there, I got his room number, and then it was game time. I was nervous and didn't know why. I walked into the room with my head held high. I didn't want to show any signs of weakness.

"This is a nice surprise," he said.

It looked like he was trying to smile, but his face was so messed up that it barely moved.

"I need to know why you were following me," I said him.

"What are you talking about?" he said.

"You were following me. I want to know why?" I asked again.

"We belong together, Zinda. You are all I can think about. I love you, and I'm willing to be your baby's stepdaddy. That thug nigga that you're running behind don't love you. I doubt if he even knows what love is about. I can give you a life of peace and legal money," he said.

"How in the fuck do you know anything about him? Walking up and talking shit to somebody is not the way to start a friendship. You can't tell me shit about him because you don't know him," I told him.

He looked confused but didn't say anything. I don't get how he could say all this stuff when his dumb a.. was fighting the wrong guy in the first place. If he wanted to think Zo was my baby daddy, then why the hell would I tell him different?

"I can't believe you were on some stalker shit following me and shit. You do know that's some creepy shit, right?" I asked him.

"I wasn't trying to scare you. I just wanted to know if you were okay. That's all that was about. You have to understand when you love someone you'll do whatever you can to protect them. If you thinking I'm a creep is the result, I'm fine with that. There are too many crazy people out here looking to hurt women like you," he said.

He really thought he was looking out for me. I saw that there was nothing I could say that would make him understand how wrong he was. I never even looked at him as being anything close to a man for me. I didn't need this type of shit in my life. I had already fucked it up enough on my own, I didn't need him thinking we were a match made in heaven or nothing.

"For real, all I can do is be truthful. You ain't the one for me. I have no desire to touch you or even be in the same room with you. You don't cross my mind. I never thought of what we could be because we are all we will ever be, which is just some fucking co-workers. Don't try to contact me after this," I told him.

I couldn't tell how he felt about what I said because of how swollen his face was. I turned and walked out of the room anyway, so I never gave him a chance to respond. I thought about calling Juma and telling him what I just did, but I was sidetracked by Zo calling me.

"Hello," I answered.

"When you gonna be home?" he asked.

"Why? What's up?" I asked.

"Fuck it, never mind. You need to hurry up. You gotta pack," he said.

"Pack for what?" I asked.

This nigga ended the damn call. He didn't sound right to me. I went on to the house to see what the hell was going on now.

When I stepped in the house, him and Juma were in my living room talking. Whatever they were talking about must have been intense because the tension was thick in the room. I looked at both of them. Juma looked like he was pissed off, while Zo looked like he wanted to explain something.

"We gotta go to Virginia. Some shit happened. You don't have any choices in this, so don't cause an argument that you not gonna win. Go pack, we're leaving at midnight tonight. That's if you don't have some secret shit to do," Juma said before walking out and slamming the door.

"What was that about?" I asked Zo.

He walked out of the door shaking his head. I didn't know what was going on with them, but I knew that my ass had to pack. This was gonna be a hell of a ride with Juma and Zo both having a fucking attitude.

∞∞∞∞∞∞

A LONG ASS NINETEEN HOURS LATER, I WAS FINALLY BACK IN Virginia. I was riding with Juma while Zo and his crew followed in two cars behind us. They went to their hotel while Juma drove to his house. He unloaded the luggage while I fixed some breakfast. I knew that he was hungry from the long drive. I hopped in the shower while he ate.

After my shower, I went to the kitchen to get me something to snack on before going to bed. I was shocked to see Juma sitting at the table still with all his clothes on. He was messing with his phone, so I guess he didn't see me coming.

"Why you not dressed for bed?" I asked him.

"I ain't staying here. I just wanted to make sure you were good. You can go 'head and get in the bed. I'll lock up," he said.

He stood to his feet as if he was really going to leave.

"I thought we were gonna work on us," I told him.

"I didn't agree to that. The sad part is that I probably would have if you would have been up front with me," he said.

"Up front about what?" I asked.

"Why you go see that stalking ass nigga?" he asked me

I don't know how he found that out. I take that back. Yes, I do. I should have known that Juma and Zo still had somebody watching me.

"I just went to set the record straight with him," I told him.

"Why you ain't say shit about it?" he asked.

I couldn't answer that because there wasn't a reason for me not to tell him. I just didn't, even though I know I should have.

"Now you're standing there with that dumb ass look on your face. Check it out, you need to make a decision on if you want to stay here or go back to Florida. Whatever you decide, tell Sphynx or Key so I can set up for all your bills to be paid. We don't have shit else to discuss. You got an appointment, tell Key or Sphynx so they can get in contact with me. You not gonna be able to hit me up because I need a new phone," he said.

I looked at the phone in his hand and rolled my eyes. He looked me in the eyes with nothing but anger. He dropped the phone on the hardwood floor then stepped on it, cracking it into pieces. Then he picked it up and put it in his pocket.

"Lock the door and set the alarm. The code is your birthday," he said.

Those were the last words he said to me. He walked out the door that night, and I knew he was gone out of my life for good. I sat at the dining room table and cried like I had never cried before. This was the first time since meeting Juma that I felt this kind of pain. Through everything that we had been through, he had never looked at me like that.

CHAPTER 23

JUMA

I wanted to be mad at Zinda, I really did, but there was no need to be. She was only doing what she knew how to do, which is run from my ass. I was finally tired of chasing her or trying to get her to see what everyone else already knew. My heart was still hers, but we were never gonna be together. I wanted to give her everything that was in my power to give. The one thing I needed from her, she wasn't willing to give or even try. I needed a rider to be with me through everything. She just wasn't it.

I'm not gonna act like a nigga wasn't hurt because on some real shit, I'm hurt like a motherfucker. All she had to do was tell me why she went up there. The Florida niggas followed her, so I knew what the fuck was up. She had to learn to stop keeping shit to herself. If I tell you that this nigga been following you, why would you even go up there to see his ass? Let that nigga rot in hell.

I drove to my other house around the corner. I was never gonna be too far away from her, but she'll never know that shit. She needs to get her shit together. Whoever the next nigga is, he needs to be on his shit because she can cause a nigga to catch a hellified charge.

I went in the house and tried to get Zinda out of my head. I had a meeting to conduct tomorrow. My life was on the line. If I got out of this shit alive, then maybe I would talk to her again.

∞∞∞∞∞∞

HOW IS IT THAT I CALL A MEETING AND THE NIGGAS FROM OUT of town are on time, but the niggas that live here ain't? I was sitting at the desk spinning the gun around in a circle. Everybody was looking at me like I was crazy, but I was just waiting for Sparky to get there so we could start. I hated when people were late for meetings. If I call a meeting and you're late, we got a problem.

If you late to a meeting I call, then that shows me that you don't have any respect for me, nor do you value my time. It's a fucking embarrassment that we have folks here from out of town on time, but the local mother fucker was almost twenty minutes late. My crew knew how I felt about that shit.

Everybody looked up when the door opened, and Sparky walked in looking high as the fucking moon.

"My bad, Juma," he said.

I gave his ass a head nod to make him think shit was cool. He walked closer to me, and that's when I picked the gun up and shot him in the throat.

"Okay, now we can start the meeting," I said and stood up.

"Juma, you got this man bleeding on the floor," one of the guys said.

"He good. He doesn't need that blood. Like I was about to say, y'all get to know each other, exchange numbers, and all that good shit. These guys are from Florida, they're gonna help us get rid of the problem we been having.

"Now, if you see them out on the street, act like you never seen them before unless they with me. Just know they down with us no matter what. Don't get no bright ideas either because you will end up like this nigga here," I told them.

I didn't need to tell them details because that shit was above they pay grade. The fewer of them that knew what was about to go down was better for us. So, if you weren't involved in what had to go down, then you didn't need to know.

"Call the cleanup niggas to come get this nigga. Oh yeah, y'all see what happens when you come to a meeting late?" I asked.

I didn't need an answer. I knew my point was made. I left before the cleanup crew got there. I didn't get much sleep last night, so my next stop would be a bar to get something to drink. I took out my back up phone, and it had messages and missed calls from Key and Sphynx. I wasn't in the mood to discuss Zinda, so I tossed it in the passenger seat and went to the closest bar.

I was sitting there for about half an hour when Sphynx came up and sat beside me. I just looked at him and shook my head. I didn't want to hear how I needed to talk to Zinda or none of that other bullshit. I wasn't gonna speak first. That nigga knew what the deal was.

"She's in the hospital. After you left last night, she got so upset she started throwing up, then she passed out. The ambulance came and got her. She's at General hospital now. They gonna keep her for a few days for observation," Sphynx said.

"Oh yeah? That shit sucks. I hope she pulls through," I said.

"Man, you're tripping. She's carrying your seed, and that's all you can say?" he fussed.

"She only here because I made her come. You forgot she took her ass all the way to fucking Florida. Okay, check it out, what room she in?" I asked.

"623. Maybe she got Baby Brain. You should check it out," he said.

"What the hell is that? Man, don't be making up shit just to make it seem like it's a reason for her to be doing all this dumb shit," I told him.

He laughed at me like what I said was crazy or something. I ain't never heard of no bullshit like that, so I was looking at his ass the same way.

"I went and talked Key's doctor about how she was being all moody and shit. Come to find out, it's a side effect with some pregnancies. He also told me about this shit called Baby Brain.

It's when they can't focus on stuff, real sensitive like crying all the time, and they forgetful as fuck," he said.

"Yeah, alright. Well her Baby Brain ass is gonna make me kill her ass. It's best that we keep our distance from each other," I told him.

"If you say so, but you gonna have to see her. She all fucked up, man. If she keeps going like this, the stress is gonna make her lose the baby. Then, who you gonna blame?" he asked.

"I'm gonna blame her pickle head ass because she started this shit," I told him.

"If you say so. I know that damn baby gonna be hard headed as fuck. Between the two of y'all, they gonna have to be home-schooled for trying to fight the damn teacher in preschool." Sphynx laughed.

I didn't find the shit funny, but I nodded my head. We sat there and threw back a few more. There was a baseball game on, so we watched that 'til it went off, then we went our separate ways. I got in the car and made a phone call.

"Edible Arrangements, Lisa speaking," the lady answered.

"Yes, I have a friend in the hospital. Do you have any get well arrangements available?" I asked.

"Yes, we do?"

"Can you throw in the biggest teddy bear y'all have with a bunch of balloons with it?"

"Yes, we can. There is a card. Would you like to add a personal message?"

"Yeah, sure. Can you put on the card the following message? Sit the fuck down somewhere. If you lose my baby, I'm fucking you up. That's real nigga shit. Play with it."

"Umm, well, okay," she said.

"Can you read that back to me?" I asked her.

I was just fucking with her, but she did it anyway. I was cracking up at how the little white girl sounded repeating the message. I paid for the order, gave her the delivery information, and went home. I turned my phone off because I knew my phone would be blowing up soon.

I was pulled out of my sleep by my door being beat on like it was about to be knocked down. I grabbed my glock from off the nightstand. I didn't bother putting any clothes on because evidently whatever the person needed was urgent.

"What the fuck?" I asked when I opened the door.

"What the fuck is your problem? You got my sister bawling her eyes out, and you won't even come to the hospital to check on her," Key fussed.

She walked right past me like I didn't have a gun in my hand. I'm standing there in my boxer briefs, and she was trying to lay my ass out about her dumb ass sister.

"Bruh, you're waking me up behind your sister. She knows I'm not fucking with her like that. Why is it a shock that I didn't come to the hospital?" I asked.

"You still love her, right?"

"Yeah, I doubt if I'm gonna stop. She's playing too many games. She's gonna make me kill her ass. I chose to walk away instead of being locked away," I told her.

"She loves you, Juma," Key said.

"Are you asking or telling me?" I asked her.

"You know she does, why you tripping? She's a mess in the hospital," Key told me.

"If she loves me, then why is she making every fucking thing hard as fuck? Everything, she's fighting me on. It doesn't matter how big or small it is, she stay against me. You need to be talking to her ass and letting me sleep. I'm not saying I don't love her, but she doesn't love me enough to try to make shit work. It takes two, Key, not one and a fucking possible. This ain't spades."

Key just looked at me with that nigga please look. She could talk 'til she was blue in the face. I wasn't changing on shit I had to say. I wasn't fucking with Zinda like that no more.

"Okay. well I'll keep you updated since you're acting like a female these days," Key said.

I gave her a head nod.

"Lock the door on your way out," I told her.

I went to my room to try to get some sleep.

CHAPTER 24

ZO

"**W**hat kind of nigga you got us working with up here?" Boot asked me.

Boot was one of the guys that I brought up there with me. I knew the question was coming because they had all been quiet since the meeting yesterday. I was getting a lot of side eyes, even though I told them that Juma was not the nigga to be crossed. This was his shit, and he ran it the way he saw fit.

"Man, he a cool ass nigga till you make that other side come out. Real shit, he intense about shit that means something to him. Just do what you supposed to do, and you'll be fine. Make sure you early for meetings too," I threw in there to be funny.

He shook his head. We were used to niggas dying, that wasn't the problem. The problem was that the nigga died because he was late to a meeting. That shit was fucking wild as hell. It was funny to me, but everybody else thought the nigga was crazy.

"Look there go a nigga that wasn't at the meeting," Moe said.

I pulled up to ol' boy and got the show on the road.

"Aye, young blood, me and my boys just moved up here from Florida, and we trying to get put on. Do you know who's the person to talk to 'bout some shit like that?" I asked.

He looked at us like he was trying to decide if we were legit or not.

"If you ain't the man, then just say that. No need to have us standing here like you thinking about the shit. Either you know, or you don't know. What the fuck is there to think about?" Moe said.

"What's y'all names?" he asked.

"You don't need our names to fucking answer a question," Moe said.

"Aye, you can't be rolling up here talking all crazy. Your niggas need my help, not the other way around," he said.

"What one nigga don't know, another one will," Moe said.

I just let this shit play out because in a way I wanted to know what ol' boy was built like. Moe had already disrespected him by talking crazy for no damn reason. Not once did he try to put Moe in his place. We were the niggas from out of town, how you gonna let us roll up like this talking shit?

"I need y'all names and numbers, so I can give it to the next man in charge. He gonna check y'all out. If y'all check out, he'll call ya," he said.

"I don't need the next man in charge I need the one running shit," I told him.

"The one running shit is on his way to a dirt retirement. Like I said, you need the next one in charge. Are you gonna leave the info or not?" he asked.

"If he ain't pushing no bullshit or on some other shit, give him this info," I told him.

I gave him the info he asked for then we walked to the car. As I pulled off, I saw him look at the license plates and write it down. That's exactly what we wanted him to do. When he checked my shit, everything would come up matching. The best part of it was Moe's old lady worked at the DMV in Florida. Once one of our plates got put in the system, it was going to be flagged. Once it was flagged, it would show who was looking into our shit. That's the first step to finding out who was after Juma, and they didn't even know it.

∞∞∞∞∞∞

I WAS SITTING AT THIS DAMN HOSPITAL CHECKING ON ZINDA. She was going off about some shit Juma had sent to the hospital instead of bringing his ass up there to check on her. I found the shit funny because everybody knew they were gonna be married soon, and she was gonna be knocked up again as soon as possible.

"Why he treating me like I don't matter? You a nigga, so I know you know the answer. Y'all all fucking buddy-buddy now, so let me guess, you not gonna say nothing against yo homie," Zinda said.

"Why you being extra? You make that man crazy just like he makes you crazy. Y'all need to fuck y'all problems away, if you ask me," I told her.

"Why you so nasty? Fucking ain't the answer all the time," she said.

"Shit, that's what your ass say. Think about it. Fucking causes the raw emotions to come out. You be so wrapped up in the pleasure your body is feeling that you can't do shit but tell the truth. Your concentration is all fucked up, so you can't think of a lie," I told her.

She looked at me like she was surprised that what I just said made sense. I don't know why she thought I was dumb or something. Just like I wasn't dumb enough to try my hand with her confused ass when I saw her.

"Real shit, you need to stop holding shit over his head that he didn't have shit to do with. You too worried about him possibly hurting you that you gonna miss out on an epic love all together," I told her.

"I'm trying to get back to us, but he not talking to me. I don't even have his phone number. He broke the phone that I had the number to in my face the last time I saw him. He wants me to send messages by Key or Sphynx to him," she said.

She had tears running down her face. She wasn't boo whooing or ugly crying, but I could see the pain on her face. I wanted to say something to help her feel better, but fuck, I had no clue of what the hell to say. Even though I looked out for her, and it was like she was a sister, she really wasn't. I didn't feel right just saying some off the wall shit to her.

"Y'all will work it out, trust me," was all I could say.

There was a light knock on the door, then it opened. There were two niggas that I had never seen before. I knew it was about to be some shit because they looked at me like they wanted to drop my ass on sight. I'm not a small nigga by far, but one of them was dark skinned and built like he lifted weights in his sleep. The other was brown skinned, he was a little smaller, but I knew he was with the shits too.

Why is this girl surrounded by all these violent ass niggas? I cursed under my breath because I left my piece in the fucking car, and I was there alone. *Fuck.*

"Who the fuck is this? Where the fuck is Juma? I know that's Juma baby you're carrying, so again, who the fuck is this?" the dark-skinned guy asked.

Zinda was sitting there crying and not saying shit. The other guy walked up on me. I stood up because I was not trying to give his ass no advantage. These Virginia niggas like to sneak mother-fuckers.

"Who the fuck is you?", he asked.

"I'm Zo. I'm a friend of Zinda and Juma," I told him.

"You not from here?" the dark-skinned guy asked.

"Nah, I'm from Florida," I answered.

The dark-skinned guy took out his phone while the other pulled his glock out. He held it in my face while the other nigga made the phone call.

"Y'all stay doing shit, but everybody wonder why I left like I did. Jabba, get that gun out of his face. What are y'all doing? He told y'all he knows Juma, and Juma knows him. Why all the extra shit?" Zinda fussed.

"Do Juma know you in here crying in front of this nigga? He the reason why you're crying?" the nigga named Jabba asked.

"Juma is the reason I'm crying. You and Raheem's crazy asses are the reason my pressure is going up," she fussed.

I could tell she was mad, but she wasn't yelling or none of that.

"Juma, we up here to see lil sis, and it's some Florida nigga up here chilling. It's just them two, you know this nigga like that?" the guy on the phone said.

I shook my head because I don't know what type of pussy these Virginia chicks had, but I wanted no parts of this bullshit. He said a few more words and hung up the phone.

"Put it up, Jabba, he straight," he said then he looked at me. "Welcome to the team, man, I'm Raheem. This anger management dropout is Jabba. We were the plugs before we passed the shit down. 'Preciate the shit you're doing with Juma. You didn't have to agree to the shit. One day we should all go out with your team for drinks and shit," Raheem said.

"No doubt. Me and my team will be there, just let me know when. I'm gonna get out of here, though. I'll call you later, Z," I said.

"Hey man, my bad with the gun and all that. We done had some shady ass bitch niggas trying they hand lately. We a tight clique, and we don't trust too many. We damn sure don't trust them around our women," Jabba said.

"Me and Juma not together!" Zinda yelled.

I could do nothing but laugh because she was just sitting there crying behind the nigga.

"See, even this nigga know that's bullshit coming out of ya mouth. You said ya name Zo, right?" Raheem asked. I nodded my head. "Sit down, I gotta set her ass straight on some shit. Send a text to your crew and let them know to meet you at a spot called Spades in Virginia Beach in an hour and a half. You can leave out with us when I'm done with this piece of work here," Raheem said.

I know he wasn't fucking around by the sound of his voice. Jabba went and sat down in a chair on the other side of the room. I didn't know these niggas like that, but I also knew the rep they had, so I sat my ass down. I ain't no punk, but I ain't stupid either. I sent the text, and that's when he started talking.

"You know I should slap the fuck outta you, right? You knew that nigga was in love with you before you opened ya fucking legs and fucked the nigga's common sense out. Did you really think he wouldn't come find your ass? You got this nigga buying whole apartment buildings and shit, but you confused on if he loves you or not. Don't look all sad and shit. You knew what the deal was when you saw me. You gonna keep playing with him, and he gonna kill your ass, straight the fuck up. Then I gotta explain to your midget ass sister that this is the bed you made. Her crazy ass gonna try to kill Juma, then Imma have to shoot her then kill Sphynx. If I kill him, Serion gonna come for me, then your kids gonna be fucking orphans and shit," he said.

"Stay on topic, nigga," Jabba said.

All these motherfuckers are crazy as fuck.

"Fuck you man? She gets the fucking point," Raheem said.

"Z, all he trying to say is. Both of y'all wrong as fuck. Trust me, I ain't saying I'm perfect with all the shit that me and Tee done been through, but at the end of the day, I ain't shit without her. Y'all too busy running from shit to see how good y'all are for each other. I don't know if it's pride, ego, or just being stubborn as fuck, but y'all need to cut this shit out.

"He can't focus on the streets, and you in the damn hospital hooked up to all this bullshit. For what? You left and went to Florida just to end up back here. You pregnant, and on top of that, you crazy pregnant, so you need your family around you. The next time you pick up and leave, you won't have to worry about Juma because I'm gonna come get your ass my damn self," Jabba told her.

She didn't talk back, just sat there listening to what they were saying. I guess they were the oldest out of everybody because she was sitting there like she got caught with his hand in the cookie jar.

"Raheem, I tried to tell him that I was sorry. I want to work on us, but now he's not dealing with me at all. He even sent a fucked up get-well card when he found out I was here. He hasn't brought his ass up here at all, not even a fucking phone call. Look at this shit," she said, giving him the card.

He took the card, and a smile came across his face. I admit the shit was funny, but it was still fucked up for him to do to the woman he loved. I wasn't gonna laugh in her face, though.

"Nigga, this shit is your fault. You the one that made Juma like he is. You and that fucking Jinx. This got y'all name written all over it. Now I gotta go play Dr. Phil, cuz this nigga gonna fuck around and catch a charge while he trying to be hard. Then she gonna go out here and try to date some clown, then he gonna kill the nigga. All because of you and fucking Jinx," Raheem fussed.

I didn't know who Jinx was, but I could tell he was just as crazy as the rest of these niggas.

"I'm gonna talk to the nigga. Now, if I have to do an intervention with y'all, I will. Hopefully, after I talk to him, he will get his shit together. Tovina is ready to do another wedding, but y'all playing. Don't let me get Jinx retarded ass down here. That's the next step 'cause y'all wasting everybody time. Come on young blood, we gotta go find Juma ass. You can ride with us," he told me.

I didn't know if I had the option of saying no, but it didn't feel like it, so I just went with the flow. I could tell the all loved each other, but they were all still crazy as fuck.

CHAPTER 25

JUMA

I don't know what it was, but every time I tried to sleep, niggas always wanted to come bang on the door. I got up to drag my drunk ass to the door. Yeah, I was hung over from drinking all fucking night.

I opened the door to see Raheem, Juma, and Zo looking at me all crazy. I shook my head because I knew what this shit was about. Raheem was on his preaching shit. I swear that nigga needed to be a preacher instead of the fucking plug.

"Sup," I said.

I turned and left they ass at the door. They got the hint and came in behind me. I went to the fridge and got my orange juice out so I could drink out the carton.

"Nigga, you not gonna ask us if we want something to drink?" Raheem said.

I held out the carton, but they all declined it. I shrugged my shoulders because I wasn't gonna beg them to get any.

"What's up?" I asked.

"We just saw Zinda," Raheem said.

"Word," I responded.

I mean they just called me not too long ago asking about Zo, so I already knew they saw her.

"You not gonna ask how she's doing?" Raheem said.

"I don't have to. Y'all not all fucked up, so I know she not dead. I'm not beat for the details. If she still alive and the baby good, that's all I need to know," I told them.

Raheem shook his head. Zo was looking around like he didn't know why he was there.

"Okay, so you good if another nigga is digging up in her pussy? Kissing all on her titties while he's finger fucking her. Running his fingers through her hair while she's topping him off?" Jabba asked.

I wanted to front and tell him yeah, I'm good with all that, but I couldn't. I took another drink from the juice to keep from cussing this nigga out.

"Speak up, I can't hear ya, nigga," Jabba said.

"If that's what she wants, I can't say shit about it," I said.

The carton bent, and juice got all on the floor.

They started laughing.

"Calm your ass down. The juice carton not fucking Zinda. You ain't have to kill it," Raheem said laughing.

"What do y'all want, man?' I asked.

"You need to sit down with Zinda and get y'all shit together. You know you love her and she loves you," Raheem said.

"Love ain't enough sometimes, and this is one of those times," I told him.

"You wanna be like Serion out here looking crazy 'cause you don't trust chicks no more? What if she finds some nigga that's willing to do the most in a good way? How you feel about ya kid living in the house with another nigga? Think about it. She not gonna stay single just so you won't get in your feelings," Raheem said.

"Nigga, we saw that fucked up get well card. You know that would push her to go fuck some nigga on some get back shit. You need to go see the damn girl for real. She says she okay, but she doesn't look okay. She look like she could pass out any minute. You gonna kill the damn girl from stress, then you gonna have to raise a kid by ya self. You ready for that shit?" Jabba asked.

I looked at these niggas to see if they were serious.

"Where the fuck was this 'don't fuck up ya love life' seminar when she hauled ass to Florida? Everybody was home fucking they wives when her retarded ass dipped for no fucking reason. Regardless of how pitiful she looked, she started this shit," I told them.

I was fucking tired of everybody telling me what I needed to do. I mean, what did she need to do? Did they tell her that dumb shit?

"Get the fuck out," I told them.

I know they were my niggas and shit, damn near my older brothers, but this shit here wasn't up for discussion. Zinda could do what the fuck she wanted. She didn't have to worry about me.

I should have known these niggas was gonna try me. Jabba retarded ass pulled his fucking gun on me.

"You not gonna be ready to understand till you push her ass to wig the fuck out on you," Jabba said.

He took his shirt and pulled it up. He pointed at a scar.

"You see this shit? You wanna know where it came from. Tee's crazy ass. We broke up, and she ran up on me with some bitch in the car. Her crazy ass shot me, talking 'bout the girl wasn't her problem, but I was. After she shot me, she took me to her house and stitched my ass up. The crazy part is she cried because she didn't wanna see me in pain," he said.

"His point is, when you push a chick that far, you know they love you. Zinda is way worse than Tee, so imagine what she's gonna do when you push her," Raheem said.

I couldn't see Zinda shooting me. They can talk all that good shit.

"Just go see her today. She looks like shit for real. You can walk in and out, but go see her," Jabba said.

"I'll go check her out if that gets y'all out of my damn house," I told them.

"Alright, you handle yo business. We going to Spades to chill out and get some drinks," Raheem said.

I guess that was my cue to put my clothes on, go see Zinda, then meet them at Spades. Raheem was a complicated ass nigga, but I knew how he moved by now.

I gave them a head nod, they left, and I went to put my damn clothes on. I guess sleep would have to wait.

∞∞∞∞∞∞

I WALKED INTO THE HOSPITAL ROOM AND SOME NIGGA WAS IN there laughing and kee-keeing with Zinda. I didn't go off, I just walked in and sat my ass in the first empty seat I saw.

"Well, I'll be back to check on you before my shift ends," the nigga said.

"Okay," she said, smiling all hard and shit.

"How are you? My name is Clarence. I'm the nurse on duty tonight. I will leave y'all two to talk and spend time. See you later, Z," he said.

I didn't even look his way. My eyes were focused on Zinda. He got the hint and left.

"What's up?" I asked her.

"I know you're only here because Raheem and Jabba forced you to be here. You can go 'head and leave. I'll tell them you came by, spoke to me, and left," she said.

She was looking everywhere but at me. I saw a tear drop from her face, and I couldn't make my mouth say the smart shit that I wanted to. I really looked at her. She had bags under her eyes, and she just looked fucking tired. I don't know for sure if all of that was because of me, but I knew most of it was. I sat on the side of the bed and put my hand on her stomach.

I don't know what made me do that, but when I did, I felt some shit run through me. She was carrying my seed, but I was so busy trying to make her feel like she made me feel when she left that they were in the hospital. She was in there because of me and that dumb ass argument.

I'm not excusing the shit that she did because she had a bunch of rocks for a brain, if you ask me. Even still, she was the mother of my first child, the beginning of my lineage. On top of that, she had my heart and my mind going crazy.

I leaned over and kissed her stomach. Once I did that, I couldn't stop. I had been up for days trying to drink the memories of her away. Seeing her like this, I knew without a doubt that she was hurting as much as I was. If she was hurting, then my child was hurting. Right now, I only wanted to take the pain away.

I licked the dark line that went from her belly button to her pussy. I could hear her calling my name, but right now I was focused and busy. We could talk after, but right now wasn't no talking happening. When I got to the pussy I hadn't seen in months, I was happy as fuck that she shaved, but I was gonna have to ask her who she was keeping it clean for.

I didn't bother with separating her pussy lips with my fingers or none of that. I put the whole damn thing in my mouth. I sucked on both lips while my tongue went to find her clit.

When I tell you she had the best tasting pussy ever, that was a fucking understatement. She started rubbing on my head and shit like it was a crystal ball or something, but I didn't give a fuck. She started moaning and cussing like she was crazy. The machines she was hooked up to started going off.

"Bae, they gonna come in here," she moaned.

I don't know why she was telling me that shit. I heard them shits, just like she did, but I wasn't stopping. Whoever came in there was getting a show today. Fuck what she thought. The door swung open, and Mr. Fruit Cake nurse was standing in the door.

I spread her pussy wide open and started licking her shit real fast. He was standing there stuck. I kicked it up a notch. I slid my index finger and my middle finger inside her, started massaging her g spot. She got to squirming and shit. I knew I had her ass. She started screaming my name and shit as she fed me the only dinner that I'd been craving since the last time I had some of her. When she finished cumming all over my face, I stood up and kissed her right in the mouth.

See, Zinda was a straight freak when it came to us. I knew she didn't mind nurse cupcake looking at us because he still hasn't moved. He was sitting there stuck like a mother fucker. She was licking her juices off my face and kissing me all sloppy and shit.

While we were kissing, I pulled my joggers and boxers down. I stepped out of them because I was gonna fuck the shit out of her ass. One, because we had a fucking audience. Two, because like I said, I been craving her ass. She been stressing me out, so she was about to get all the stress she caused.

"Get your ass against the fucking wall," I told her.

She got up to go to the wall, and I yanked the dumb ass hospital gown off her. She was facing the wall when I started kissing her on the back of her neck. I lifted her hands above her head.

"Leave them there," I told her.

She only moaned a response, but I knew she understood. I kissed and bit her back on my way down to my knees. I kissed both of her ass cheeks. The baby had them spread all out and juicy and shit. Before I could stop myself, I spread them motherfuckers apart and for the first time in my life, I ate some ass. I ate that shit like my life depended on it. She was screaming and shit, so I guess I was doing it right.

I stood up and slid in her pussy. When I tell you, a nigga got emotional as fuck, nigga. That shit had never ever happened to my ass before. I started smacking her ass and going ham in that pussy.

"You're bringing your ass home," I said as I kept smacking her ass and fucking her.

"YES!" she screamed.

"I love you, Zinda. You gonna marry me, you hear me. It's me and you. Stop with the bullshit!" I yelled.

I stopped smacking MY ass and gripped the fuck out of it. I rammed myself inside her over and over. I was so gone that I didn't hear shit. It was like I was having an out of body experience or something.

After I finally came inside her, I helped her get back in the bed. She looked at me with a confused expression.

"Juma, you're crying," she said.

I didn't know I was until she said, it but once she said it, I couldn't stop. I got in the bed with her, and we cried together. I mean we were fucking ugly crying together. It was like we were both letting go of all the bullshit from the past couple of months.

I knew then that we were both done with the petty shit. From here on out, it was just us, and that's all that mattered.

CHAPTER 26
ZO

Juma never met us the other night at the bar, but I was cool with that. I knew him and Zinda had some shit to iron out. I hope they got their shit together, but only time will tell. We had been texting back and forth talking about this mystery nigga. He called me, but his voice was disguised, which made me think it was somebody that Juma knew.

He never said Juma's name, but he kept talking about some nigga that couldn't run the streets no more. There was something off about the first conversation, but I couldn't put my finger on it.

My crew was supposed to meet the so-called next nigga in charge at some white titty bar. I told the guys to keep their eyes open because I knew something was gonna happen tonight, I just didn't know what it was. When we were on the phone, the person told me that I could bring my crew, but the negotiations were to be made by me and them, one on one in one of the back rooms. I couldn't bring my phone or anything with me in the back room.

I was cool with that because all I needed to do was see a face. I came all the way up there to see a face, and that's what I was gonna do.

We walked in, and just like I figured, there were a bunch of white females with no titties and no asses. I had never seen bull-shit like this in my life, but this was what they called a titty bar. I took a seat and looked around. We were the only ink spots in the room.

"Man, what the fuck you done got us in? We the only niggas in here. Make sure you don't see any rope anywhere. We all 'bout to be swinging by our necks," Moe said.

I was trying to see everybody's face that was in the place. It was only about ten people in there not including us. All the folks in the place were too busy whispering and looking at us to pay the stick figure on the stage any mind.

"Are you Zo?" a waitress asked me.

"Who wants to know?" I asked.

"I was sent over here to tell you the person you're waiting on will meet you in room 4. It's down the hall on the right. I'll entertain your friends," she said with a smile.

The fellas looked at her and started laughing.

"I don't mean no harm snowflake, but your lips and legs let me know that if you suck my dick or try to fuck me, we liable to start a fire in this joint. My thick ass wood and your twigs for legs and branches for lips will damn sure start a spark if they rub together. We good on the entertainment. Just bring us a pitcher of soda. I know y'all liquor watered down like a mother fucker," Moe said.

I shook my head and got up to head for the room. I tried to remember the layout of the building for when we come back to shoot this country shit up. I walked in the room and was shocked to see a bitch sitting on the couch. I looked around the room then at the number on the door to make sure I was in the right spot.

"You can come in, you're in the right place, sexy," she said.

I looked at her with her fire red hair and light skin. She kind of looked like Charlie Baltimore, but I knew it wasn't her. She was sexy as fuck, but why the hell was she in there was my question.

"You're the next in charge?" I asked.

"Yeah, but I have to finish making somebody's life a living hell first. When I'm not being entertained by seeing the dog run after its own tail, I'll shoot it and put it out of its misery. Until then, I'll enjoy the show," she said.

"What gives? I mean, why you want to be that nigga so to speak?" I asked.

"Well, I've been around enough ballers, dope boys, and plugs to know the ins and outs of most of the operations around here. Niggas tend to pillow talk when you can run ya tongue across their nut sack with their dick past ya tonsils. I was fine being an armpiece until the one I was supposed to sit on the throne with pushed me to the side for a bitch that was making him look like fucking clown.

Now he's running around trying to find a nigga that don't fucking exist. The shit is epic. It makes my pussy wet just to think about it," she said.

Zinda's gonna blow this bitch's head off.

"If you got everything figured out, why take me up on my offer to bring us in?" I asked.

"Well, because I needed to see the nigga who fucked up my cousin," she said.

"Cousin? I don't know you, so who the hell is your cousin?" I asked.

"Kenny," she said.

I guess she saw me connecting the dots in my head because she smiled.

"I see you're smart. Are you smart enough to take me up on my proposition?" she asked.

"What is that?" I asked.

"Well," she said.

She got up and started walking around the room. I knew what she was trying to do. She wanted me to focus on her ass and titties that she had jiggling everywhere for me to just agree to anything. She was definitely underestimating me and my ties to Juma and Zinda. I couldn't wait to tell his ass that this shit was behind a scorned chick.

"I want you to run shit for me. To be my right hand, so to speak. Once the current establishment is brought down I want us to be a team. What do you say?" she asked.

"Okay, how do you know my loyalties don't lie with Juma and his crew?" I had to ask.

"If they did, you wouldn't have gotten his bitch pregnant," she said.

"She doesn't wanna be with me, though," I said.

Hey, if her dumb ass wanted to go off her stalking ass cousin's word, who was I to tell her super smart dumb ass any different?

"You won't mind killing them both then," she said. "I've been trying to get close enough to him to kill him, but he ain't fucking with me at all. He's only trying to love that bitch, when I could have been the Bonnie to his Clyde. Instead, he's running around behind her like Forrest Gump was running behind that hoe Jenny," she fussed.

I guess crazy as fuck was a family trait.

"What do you say? Are you gonna run the world with me, sexy?" she asked.

"Yeah, I'm in. What's your name, Queen?" I asked.

"Cherry, just call me Cherry, baby," she said.

CHAPTER 27
JUMA

I was sitting there watching Zinda sleep. Since coming there the other day and fucking the shit out of her, we had been good. I knew this wouldn't be the end of the BS. In fact, the shit was just beginning. I talked to the fellas, and now it was time for me to tell Zinda what was really going on.

I knew that there was a chance of her going the fuck off and screaming that her hands weren't pregnant. I needed her and her sister to go into killer mode.

"Babe, I need you to do something for me. I need you to kill Kenny. I know you pregnant and shit, but you the only one that can do it," I told her.

"Okay, just let me know when," she said.

I was expecting her to ask why or something, but she didn't.

"You not gonna ask why?" I asked her.

"No need to. He's been a problem for a while, so I get it. It's gonna have to wait until I get out of here," she said.

"You sure you up to it?" I asked her.

"Yup, I got it, babe," she told me.

I gotta admit my dick got kind of hard hearing her agree to that. Shit been so lopsided with us lately, and it feels good for us to be on the same page. I hated that I had to leave her tonight to go iron out some details. Zo called and told me that he has some killer ass news. Me and Sphynx were going to meet him while

Key stayed with Zinda. I couldn't help but wanna fuck her right now, but that would have to wait.

∞∞∞∞∞∞

WE GOT TO THE HOTEL ROOM WHERE ZO AND THEM WERE staying, and I braced myself to hear that I had to kill the girls' pops or something. He was the only one that I could think of who would come for me like this. I just needed proof.

I knew he still reached out to Key, although she hasn't taken a call or returned a text yet. I'm sure he's dialed the old number for Zinda too. She never brought him up, so I didn't either.

"What's going on? So when we gotta kill Esposito?" I asked him.

"Who the fuck is Esposito?" Zo asked me.

"I thought you said you knew who was doing all this shit and after me," I said.

"Cherry," he told me.

He sat back and looked at me. Sphynx looked at me too.

"Hold the fuck up, Cherry who?" I asked, standing up.

"The same Cherry that you made suck your dick in the club. I told your ass you were wrong for that shit," Sphynx said.

"Charlie Baltimore look alike?" I asked to be clear

"Hell, yeah that's her. She's pissed with your ass, nigga. Evidently, she feels like she should be with you not Zinda. She says she your Bonnie, nigga. Since you didn't choose her, she gonna be my Bonnie, and we gonna run the streets," Zo told me.

I wanted to go to that bitch house and put two bullets in her forehead.

"What Kenny got to do with this? How he fit in?" I asked.

"That nigga her cousin. You done pissed off the craziest family ever. You the real MVP," Zo said and laughed.

Him and Sphynx were gonna have jokes for days, I already knew that. Right now, the shit ain't funny at all. If this shit doesn't make a nigga wanna be faithful, nothing will. I don't even think I fucked her ass I think she just sucked me off. How the fuck was I supposed to know she had dope girl dreams while she was sucking me off.

"How do she know about my houses and shit?" I asked.

"She been loving the crew, dog. The boys are out taking care of the niggas that was working with her now. I'm 'bout to call her over here. She supposed to come over tonight so we can consummate our arrangement. What y'all wanna do?" Zo asked me.

"When is that nigga Kenny coming into town?" I asked.

"He on his way up. You supposed to die this weekend," he answered.

"Fuck you, nigga," I said, giving him the finger.

Zo was texting on his phone and laughing. I knew he was texting Cherry's dumb ass.

"She on her way up," Zo said.

Sphynx looked at me and started laughing. I didn't know we was killing her ass tonight, but oh well.

"Go in the closet, Sphynx," I said.

"Nigga, I ain't R. Kelly. What the fuck I look like in a closet?" he said.

"I'm getting under the bed. Bring her over her so she can get on her knees to suck you off. I got it from there," I told him.

I had a trick for her ass tonight.

"I don't even want to know," Sphynx said.

He walked in the bathroom while I slid under the bed. She knocked on the door.

It was showtime.

"Hey, now once we do this, you not gonna get mad cause I don't return a text in ten minutes, right? You not the type of chick I want to get pissed at my black ass," Zo said.

"You don't have to worry about that. We gonna have the streets on lock. You gonna be down with a real Queen," Cherry said.

"You did that shit nice. I mean how you had niggas hitting Juma spots and shit. How you come up with that shit by yourself?" Zo asked.

"Niggas just don't know, strippers be listening when they be talking in the club. Never conduct business at the club. Always remember that," Cherry told him.

"I hear that shit. I guess you learn something new every day. Let me see what kind of head game you got that make a nigga wanna turn on his squad," Zo said.

I felt him sit on the bed. I saw her get down on her knees. He was sure to have his legs wide enough for me to get a shot off. She was so busy trying to pull his dick out that she never heard me take the safety off the gun. I aimed it right at the front of her pussy and let off a shot.

"Ahhhhh!" she screamed.

I got from under the bed, stood over her, and shot her in the face three times. Once in the mouth and two to the head. Sphynx came out of the bathroom, and saw her on the floor with four holes in her, and laughed.

"Nigga, did you have to shoot her in the pussy?" he asked laughing.

"Yeah," I told him.

"You do know her cousin is coming in tonight. What we gonna do?" Zo asked.

"Sphynx, do Key got her piece with her?" I asked.

"Now nigga, you know she do. Knowing her, she got more than one. What's up?" he asked.

"Call her and let her know Kenny coming they way. They need to either kill him before we get there or hold his ass," I told him.

He got on the phone. I took Cherry's phone and sent a text message to Kenny's number asking where he was. He said he just got to Norfolk. I told him to go see Zinda and gave him her room number. I made some excuse up 'bout her having a customer. He said good looking out.

Now it was time for us to get her trifling ass body out of there.

CHAPTER 28

ZINDA

"We gotta kill or hold Kenny here. Sphynx just called," Key said, coming back in the room.

I thought she was in the bathroom talking freaky to Sphynx or something. I guess I was wrong this time.

"What the hell? How are we supposed to do that?" I asked

"He already in Norfolk, so we gotta think of something quick as hell. Do you have a syringe in here?" Sse asked.

"Fuck if I know. I guess it's one around here somewhere," I said.

She started looking around for one. I shook my head because I had no idea how this shit was gonna work out. There was a knock on the door. I got settled in the bed while Key stood behind the door.

This should be interesting as fuck.

Kenny came in with a smile and roses. Didn't I tell this nigga not to contact me again? Yeah, he had to die. This nigga was way past special.

"How are you doing, beautiful?" he asked.

I gave his crazy ass the stale face and rolled my eyes.

"Why are you here, Kenny? I told you not to contact me anymore. Yet here you are in my fucking hospital room. I'm not understanding you right now," I said to him.

"I got a call from my cousin letting me know that you were in the hospital. I drove right up to see about you," he said.

"Who is your cousin?" I asked.

"Cherita, you know her as Cherry. She used to mess with your ex named Juma from what she told me," he said.

"You knew who I was when I got to Florida, didn't you?" I asked.

"Yeah. I had talked to her and was telling her that this chick from VA just started at my job. We got to talking, and we figured out that she knew you. She told me I should try my hand at you. I was telling her how sexy you were and how your eyes sparkled when you laughed. That's when I started taking pictures of you and stuff," he said.

"Pictures?" I asked.

"Yeah. Check this out," he said.

He showed me his iPhone case and it was a picture of me. It was taken one day while I was at work evidently. I was not even aware that he was taking pictures of me while I was working, but here he is with a customized phone case with my fucking picture on it. I started feeling my levels of anger rise. This disrespectful son of a bitch. Who the fuck does this shit? He never got close to me. No kissing or hugging, but he was all the way gone in the head behind me. This was the creepiest shit ever.

"You do know that shit is weird as hell, right? You all in love with me, and there is no damn reason for you to be. I think you need to get some help," I told him.

"THERE'S NOTHING WRONG WITH ME! I JUST LOVE MY WOMAN WITH ALL MY HEART. YOU AND I WILL BE FOREVER!" he yelled.

I guess that was Key's cue to come from behind the door. She hit his ass in the head with a bed pan, and he stumbled a little bit. I started hitting him with the IV pole over and over again. I suddenly felt myself being lifted up, and someone snatching the pole away from me.

"Calm your ass down. You need to chill the fuck out. If you lose my baby, we gonna be beefing hard as fuck," I heard Juma say.

I was breathing hard and crying. I don't know why I was so

damn upset. I knew it would come down to this. I knew we would have to hurt his ass tonight. So why was I huffing and puffing, still ready to throw blows.

Juma wrapped his arms around me.

"That's it, bae, it's over. It's all over," he whispered in my ear.

Sphynx called for somebody to come get Kenny out of the room. Juma walked me down to the chapel. We sat there just holding each other. I stopped crying but was enjoying the closeness of Juma. My eyes were closed, but I could feel him slip a ring on my finger.

"Juma," I said, looking down at it.

"Is that a Juma yes or a Juma no?" he asked.

"That depends on the question," I said with a smile.

"Will you be the only chick to get this hurricane tongue and big ass dick long as you alive?" he asked.

"Yes, I will," I told him.

He kissed me like he's never kissed me before. For the first time in a long time, I decided that it was time to stop running. I'm glad I did because I was about to be the wife of a crazy ass nigga. I had to pray for our baby because they were gonna be all fucked up. My attitude and Juma's attitude, that child was about to stay in trouble.

The head nurse on the floor knew what had gone down, but she agreed to keep things quiet if Zo took her on a date. The funniest thing ever was to see his face when she said what he had to do. It didn't take long for him to understand what was at risk. We couldn't have the police up there asking a bunch of questions and shit.

"I don't know about these Virginia females. Y'all niggas be moving like y'all under a spell or something. I'm not trying to be like y'all," Zo said.

"Nigga it ain't about being a Virginia female. We just the right type of females to handle these niggas. It takes a special woman to deal with them and their bullshit. You betta hope she's as thorough as us," Key said.

CHAPTER 29

JUMA

I could finally at least try to relax. I admit, finding out that Cherry was behind it all made me think twice about getting topped off. This was before I proposed to Zinda. I would never step out on her, so she didn't have to worry about that, but it still made me side eye all these chicks out here.

I mean, you meet a chick. Y'all fuck, or she even gives you head on the first night. Sometimes it was even in the first thirty minutes of meeting her. How can she expect to be cuffed by anybody? Even the nigga with lent in his pockets want to have a chick that don't carry herself as a cum dump.

I still had Cherry's phone, so I sent a text out to her crew. This dumb ass hoe had a fucking group text titled *The Come-Up Crew*. I didn't have to scroll through her contacts or even try to figure out who was working with her. She was making my life easier, so I thanked her for that shit.

I sent the text out with an address and a time for us to meet them. I invited Zo's crew and my crew as well. It was time to consolidate some shit. Jabba and Raheem came too. I knew they just wanted to get in on the killing that was going to happen. It had been a minute for them, so they were excited as fuck right now.

I kept going through Cherry's phone because it was unbelievable how many niggas she was fucking. The sad part is she was doing all this fucking, but not one nigga wanted to cuff her ass. It was like everybody knew she was wide open, but damn. She had all niggas in her phone. There were only four numbers that belonged to females, and I wasn't sure that she wasn't fucking with them too.

The niggas I knew to be loyal were all texted a name of a nigga that was working with Cherry or fucking her. It was their job to kill the niggas whose names they had. This way, everybody could be taken out at once and we could get on with the meeting.

I found it funny that everyone was on time. Zo just looked at me and laughed. He really thought I was fucked up in the head. I wasn't, I just didn't care to entertain dumb shit.

"Everybody is here that we need to be here," Jabba said.

When everybody got in the room, they were all scared shitless. I had the entire floor lined with industrial plastic. It was thick as fuck, and it was best for wrapping up bodies and shit like that. I was about to start talking when Jabba's dumb ass started.

"Are y'all niggas gonna just look at the fucking plastic or can we start the meeting. If you still standing when we get out of here, I guess that means the plastic ain't here for you. If one of y'all wanna take a piss or shit because y'all scared, go 'head and do that shit. Punk ass motherfuckers," Jabba said.

I could tell who was there because they got a text from me and who was there because they got a text from Cherry's phone. I decided to let them out of their misery.

"I just want everyone to know that I found out who was behind all the dumb shit that's been going on. I also got rid of who was working with them from out of town. So, this meeting is to let y'all know that I'm back as the only nigga with the good shit. I'm branching off to open an operation in Florida as well. Zo will be in charge of that. As for the shit that Cherry was trying to set up, let's just say she underestimated a nigga," I said.

I tapped on the desk twice and everyone who had a name pulled their guns on the person they had. I laughed because a few niggas really pissed themselves once the guns were drawn.

"If you have a gun in your hand, you have proven to be loyal to the team. You have the option of staying with the team or walking away free and clear after this meeting today. Now, if you have a gun on you, that means you are disloyal, greedy, incompetent, jealous, and made the bad choice of helping Cherry. I just want you to know that you were helping that bitch all because she wanted me to cuff her ass. I didn't so, she felt like she could fuck with my shit.

"The sad part is that y'all were helping the bitch without knowing the reason why. Some of y'all got caught up because of that bomb ass mouthpiece that she had. So y'all were serving a bitch that was serving everybody she came in contact with. I wanted y'all to hear how my operation was expanding before y'all left. It's only right that y'all learn that the plan didn't work. It only just pissed me off. Most of y'all, I was feeding in the first place. If you had an issue, you should have come to me. Instead, y'all listened to a bitter bitch with a hoola-hoop for a pussy," I told them.

I knocked twice on the desk. Shots were fired, and bodies were dropped.

"Now we can go in the room across the hall and map this shit out. If you don't wanna be in on this, just walk out the front door. No pressure in this shit. If you want to remain loyal to the team, meet me across the hall," I told them.

I was happy as fuck to see that everybody came in the room. I knew going forward that I definitely had a solid team behind me. Now I have to get this meeting over with, so I can get back to my baby mama.

∞∞∞∞∞∞

"ZINDA, WHERE THE FUCK YOU AT?" I CALLED OUT AS I walked in the house.

She didn't answer me, but hearing the music blasting, I figured she didn't hear me. She always had the fucking music blasting like she was in the club or something.

I walked into the baby's nursery to see her in some booty shorts and one of my wife beaters painting the walls. She didn't want to pay people for something that she could do herself. She wasn't working, so she said she needed something to do because she would be bored at home all day.

"Yo!" I yelled.

She jumped when my voice boomed over the music. I had to laugh at her because she was so focused on what she was doing that she didn't even feel me looking at her.

"I told you about being in here like this. You didn't even know I was standing here looking at you. You gotta keep ya head on a swivel. You should know this already," I told her.

She reached in her bra and came out with a small ass gun.

"What the hell you gonna do with that little shit?" I asked.

"If I shoot you in your dick, eye, or head, it doesn't matter how small the bullet is. This is only to buy me some time, so I can get to this," she said.

She was standing there with a glock in her hand now. She got it from the crib that was in the baby's room. I knew she was always prepared, but seeing her here like this made me want to dive all in her guts. She knew damn well what I was thinking because she started laughing at me.

"Your nasty ass needs to either help me or get the hell out of my way. I have to finish painting this room. The way you're looking, I won't be able to finish today. Get out or help, those are your only two options," she told me.

I went and picked up a paint brush. I knew if I helped, the room would get done quicker. The quicker the room got done, the quicker she'd be screaming my damn name. I was all ready for getting up in her, so hey, painting is what I was doing today.

CHAPTER 30

JUMA

We were packed in the waiting room waiting on word to come back if Key had pushed my godson out yet. When I say all, I meant every fucking body. Serion, Jinx, Bam, Zo and his crew, me, Dallas, Austin, and the wives.

Sphynx and Zinda were in the delivery room with Key. Sphynx kept coming out saying he needed some air. The nigga was pale, and he was dark as a motherfucker. Everybody kept asking me if I was ready for Zinda to deliver. Hell, yeah, I was. They just didn't know I was tired as hell from dealing with Zinda and her damn pregnancy brain. If I wouldn't have known her before she got pregnant, I could swear she was a damn dingbat for real.

Some of the shit she said and did made me question a lot of shit. I had her reading Tina J and K.C. Mills books, so she would at least keep a little hood about her. The only shit about that was she wanted me to do shit like the niggas in the books. She stayed talking about them niggas. It took me a minute to figure out the niggas wasn't real. I don't know who the hell Hurricane and Yetti were, but they were the reason for a bunch of fucking arguments. I told her ass straight up if she kept talking about them niggas all sexually and shit, I was gonna go knock on Tina and K.C.'s door. We had some shit to discuss.

"He's here, he's here. My lil nigga is in the motherfucking

building!" Sphynx yelled as he walked in the waiting area.

We all clapped for him. Then we started joking on his ass. He all big and shit, but the nigga was crying his ass off.

"I'm surprised your ass didn't faint," Serion said.

"Nigga, faint for what? As open as her shit got, I told her she betta not ever whine when I'm fucking the shit out of her ass no more. If his nine-pound ass can come out of there, I know damn sure my twelve inches can get in there repeatedly," he said laughing.

I saw my baby come down the hallway, and I left them in the waiting room talking and laughing. I met her outside the door.

"You ready for lil mama to come?" I asked her.

"Yeah, if I can get put to sleep. I was in there crying for her while she was cussing out Sphynx. You should have heard them in there fussing. It was crazy. I'm gonna beg the doctor to just put me to sleep because I can't do it," she said.

The look on her face made me laugh my ass off.

"Girl, I thank the lord for you every day. I was scared as shit that we wouldn't get shit right, but we did, though. Just think, we gonna have a little you're running around," I said to her.

"Yeah, I just hope she find her an athlete or something. I would hate for her to come home saying the plug got a thing for her," she told me.

I nodded my head but stayed quiet because I be damned if my baby girl ends up with a fucking plug. She was gonna have to find her a banker or something like that. I don't want her to get a football player either. They have that CTE shit going on. One day that nigga might go off on my daughter, then I'll have to shoot his ass in the head. They won't be able to study his brain after he dies either.

"Nah, she doesn't need an athlete either. They be using steroids and shit. Those damn drugs make you go crazy and kill everybody in the house. I will kill that nigga whole fucking family," I told her.

Everybody started laughing, but I was dead ass. They kept laughing until Esposito walked his old ass in the waiting area. I looked at Zinda because I knew how she felt about her father. I didn't need her all upset.

CHAPTER 31

ZO

I'm sitting here trying to figure out how the hell I was bullied into coming to a fucking push party. Man, Zinda's ass done got eviler and aggy since she was two weeks away from her due date. She told me that I was the baby's godfather. I don't know shit about being a godfather. I knew enough to know not to fight her on it. She's been on one.

"Yo, thanks for coming, man. She would have cussed my ass out if you didn't show," Juma told me as he dapped me up.

"She texted me last night and made me send her a pic of the plane ticket," I told him and laughed.

"Yup, that sounds just like her. I don't think we're having any more after this one. I'm gonna have to knock her up and come back after the baby is born. She cried this morning because I was gonna put on a white t-shirt," he told me, shaking his head.

"A t-shirt?" I asked.

"Yeah, she been watching some shit on the Oxygen channel about gangs and shit. So, this one gang wore nothing but white t-shirts. They killed a couple niggas for wearing them. She went on and on about how I was gonna get killed, and she was gonna have to raise the baby alone. Then she tells me if I die, she gonna need a letter from me giving her permission to date," he added.

I was laughing my ass off. I could see her going off, but the look on his face was the funniest part. He looked like he was shook for real.

"You better stop talking about my sister. I'm gonna tell her, and as soon as she has the baby, we gonna jump your ass," Key said from behind us.

"Sphynx, come get Mighty Mouse. She over here threatening me again," Juma called out.

"I'm not getting in it. I'm trying to fuck when I get home tonight," Sphynx said.

"Y'all in here talking about me?" Zinda asked.

"No," we both answered together.

Sphynx, Serion, and Raheem were all laughing. They thought shit was funny, but Zinda was known to pull a knife on your ass. Juma had to take all the guns and put them up. He had them in a safe in the little barn house in the backyard. He said he put them back there because he knew she wasn't gonna walk all the way out there.

She didn't bother going back and forth with us. She went back in the kitchen with the women.

"When you gonna find you a nice chick to get locked down with?" Raheem asked.

"Never. As long as I can fuck and go home, I'm good. I don't need a woman right now, anyway. I just need to make money. I have four sisters and a mama to take care of," I told him.

"When I first met you, I bet that nigga Raheem that I was gonna have to shoot you within six months. I lost the fucking bet, so you gotta buy this nigga a dog," Jabba told me.

I looked between the two of them. I could tell by the look on his face that he was mad about losing the bet.

"You mad from losing the bet? Or, are you mad because you didn't get to shoot me?" I asked.

Jabba was off in the head, so I wanted to be sure about what he was trying to say. He was about to answer when Zinda screamed from the kitchen. We all rushed in there to see what was going on. She was bent over holding her stomach and standing in a puddle of water.

"What the fuck is that shit on the floor?" Juma asked.

"Her water broke, dummy," Key said.

"Oh shit. Zo, go get the car, I'm gonna get her bag," Juma said before hauling ass upstairs.

I went to get the car. I felt like something was wrong but prayed that everything would be okay. I know you're supposed to be in pain, but something about the way Zinda was looking didn't set right with me.

Sphynx carried Zinda to the car and put her in while Juma was right behind them with her bag.

∞∞∞∞∞∞

"JUMA, CALL MY DAD TELL HIM TO MEET US AT THE HOSPITAL," Zinda said.

"You sure?" he asked.

I even looked up in the rearview mirror. Her dad had been calling her since Key had the baby. She would never answer his calls. Now, suddenly she wants him at the hospital with us.

"Yeah, just do it," she said.

He called him right there. I, on the other hand, was praying that she would make it out of this okay. I pulled up to the hospital and hopped out to help Juma take Zinda out. Her face was a little pale, and her eyes were really glassy.

Juma lifted her out of the truck, and we looked at each other for a minute. I could tell he was just as worried as I was.

Zinda and Juma had become family to me. Seeing her with all this pain was making my ass emotional as hell. Juma and I were on shaky ground for a minute, but he was the brother I never had. He even helped me get my little sisters in line a couple of times. I needed Zinda to be okay because she deserved to be happy, and Juma would die without her.

CHAPTER 32

JUMA

I whispered in her ear that her dad was on the way. She gave me a smile.

"Tell him to stay, and I love him no matter what," she told me.

"Let me find out you gonna start being nice," I joked with her.

"Life is too short. I want him to be in the life of our child. Even if I don't make it," she said.

I nodded my head, letting her know that I understood and agreed. I walked in the bathroom after getting Zinda into a room. I told everybody that I had to use the bathroom, but I just needed a few minutes to myself.

When she got out of the car, there was blood all over the place. I looked in the mirror, and I was covered in her blood. It's not like I wasn't used to seeing a lot of blood. The fact that it was Zinda's blood is what fucked my head up.

The whole ride over there, she kept saying she didn't feel right. She said something was wrong because she felt it. I kept talking to her to try to keep her awake because she didn't look too good.

I turned on the water to try to wash some of the blood off my hands and stuff. I took my shirt off and put it in the sink. I was trying to wash some of the blood out, but it wasn't working.

"Key brought you a shirt," Zo said.

"She gotta make it, man. You saw her, man. All that fucking blood, man. I could see that something wasn't right, but there ain't shit I can do about it. I can't lose her, man. I just fucking got her for real," I told him.

"She gonna be good," he said.

I changed my shirt and walked out of the bathroom with him beside me. We got to the hallway of the room she was in. As we got closer I heard the words emergency, C-section, and some more shit.

"What the fuck is going on?" I asked as I rushed in the room.

"She's losing too much blood. We have to get her to the operating room for an emergency C-section," one of the doctors told me.

The machines started making a lot of noises. One of the nurse hopped on the bed that they had Zinda on and started doing CPR as the other pushed her down the hallway.

Seeing them working on her like that took everything out of me. I started throwing punches at the wall as tears fell freely. I heard somebody screaming that sounded like they were right behind me. I kept on punching until I couldn't punch anymore. I looked down to see my hands bleeding. I knew they should be hurting but I didn't feel anything at all. There was no pain in my hands. I could only feel the pain in my heart and soul.

"You gotta hold it together, nigga," Sphynx said.

I heard him, but nothing mattered right now but Zinda and my baby. Me holding it together was the last thing on my mind. I needed to make sure they were good.

The nurses ran over and started working on my hands while I was standing in the hallway. They were asking me questions, but I didn't understand a damn thing they were saying. They wrapped up my hands then I went to the waiting room and sat on the floor. Yeah, there were chairs that were empty, but I chose to sit on the floor. I needed her to be okay. There was no me without her. I laid on the floor and prayed that she would make it out. I needed her.

"Sir, is this all immediate family?" a doctor asked me.

"Yeah, what's going on with my wife?" I asked.

"Well, she flatlined twice. We brought her back. She lost a lot of blood, so we had to give her a transfusion. Your son is doing well. He was under distress, so we have him in the NICU for observation. He is doing good despite him coming a few weeks early. You can go see him while we get your wife settled. She isn't in a coma or anything, but she most likely will be sleep until later tonight," he said.

I slowly made my way to my feet to go see my son. I stood over his crib and just stared at him. He was so freaking small. There is no way I was picking him up until he got his weight up. I sat with him, laying my face against the glass of the bubble they had him in.

"Your wife is awake and asking for you," a nurse said.

I walked slowly behind her. For the first time in my life, I was scared to death. I walked slowly into the room. She gave me a small smile. I held her and then pulled the rest of her to me. I cried like her and my child had died. A part of me died today, the part that was more concerned with anything that didn't deal with my family. The lord had answered my prayers and kept my son and my wife out of harm's way. I had them with me, and I was going to act just like I felt. Like the luckiest man alive.

"I thought I lost y'all. I love you so fucking much Z," I told her through my tears.

"I wasn't going anywhere. I can't have you teaching my baby how to try to pull those little girls at daycare," she said.

I know she was trying to bring some light into the situation, but I didn't need to make it any lighter. I had her and my son. There was nothing better than that.

The End...

I SURE AM GONNA MISS THESE CHARACTERS

THANK YOU FOR YOUR CONTINUED SUPPORT.

Toy...

Get LiT!

*Download the LiT app today and enjoy exclusive content,
free books, and more!*

Join our mailing list to get a notification when Leo Sullivan
Presents has another release!
Text LEOSULLIVAN to 22828 to join!
To submit a manuscript for our review, email us at
submissions@leolsullivan.com

61216768R00093

Made in the USA
Columbia, SC
21 June 2019